RUBEN YGUA

A PALEOLITHIC ADVENTURE

Clans at war

All rights reserved
Ruben Ygua- 13/10/2024
Copyright ©

Contact with the author: ruben.ygua@gmail.com

The content of this work, including the spelling check, is the sole responsibility of the author.

"-We are hardly creatures molded by the whims of the climate and the environment-"

130,000 B.C., the Ice Age comes to an end and the RISS-WÜRM interglacial period begins.
Slowly, temperatures rise and the ice retreats in the northern hemisphere, abundant rains favor the formation of vast forest extensions throughout Europe and North America. A different Humanity emerges from the snows, the Neanderthal Man, perfectly adapted to the new environmental conditions, proliferates and colonizes the old continent. Also in Africa, the effects of climate change implacably affected human populations.
 The period of abundant rainfall that for 30,000 years turned Egypt and the Sahara into a paradise of lush vegetation, with abundant rivers, lakes and swamps, was now culminating. The rains had led to the first great emigration of Homo sapiens to North Africa and the Near East across the Sinai. With the end of the rains, of the four great rivers that crossed the region of the Sahara, hardly one survived, fed by the snows of the distant mountains to the south: the Nile, was being born the great desert that one day would be known as Sahara, the great herds of herbivores and the human population moved towards the last great river.
In the Near East, Homo sapiens had met for the first time with his cousin, the Neanderthal, with whom he apparently lived peacefully for millennia, as revealed by some fossils that present intermediate characteristics between Neanderthals and Homo sapiens. In spite of the differences, the abundance of resources avoided the dispute between the human groups, who no longer needed to emigrate behind the herds.
When the arid period began the living conditions of Homo sapiens and Neanderthals became difficult, a greater competition for hunting and gathering was established, and it did not take long for the first dispute for survival to take place. Numerous Neanderthals moved to southern Arabia, while Homo sapiens clans migrated east to India and Asia. However, some groups decided to cling to the land where they were born, perhaps hoping for better days.

But there were no better days... rains became scarcer and scarcer, water sources were reduced to almost disappear, vegetation no longer provided food for large herds, deserts grew in size, herbivores are scarce, large herds no longer exist, and disputes between human groups become violent, desperate.

Then, unexpectedly, new human groups emerge from the heart of Africa, bursting onto the historical scene.

THE CAVE CLAN

That morning, Arnut and his men were pleasantly surprised by one of Mother Nature's rare gifts. A lone buffalo wandered, trying to feed on the few herbs that grew on the arid meadow. Watching the group, the animal retreated, jogging into a narrow natural corridor formed between the rocky walls that cut through the mountain, a couple of kilometers away.

They were hunters with a lot of experience, in other times they used to prepare ambushes capturing a good number of large herbivores in a single hunt, which represented a meat reserve for many months. Arnut immediately understood that the characteristics of the terrain offered him a great opportunity, he knew the place, on other occasions he had captured animals by forcing them to jump to the cliff that existed at the end of the corridor. They had walked for three days without seeing any prey larger than a lizard, so the group prepared not to waste the opportunity, lit a fire where they prepared some torches, while the rest of the group was distributed in a semi-circle to prevent the escape of the animal.

It was a group of ten light-skinned hunters, punished by the harsh life outdoors, with long black hair and beards, adorned with feathers and collars of fangs and claws of animals, wearing skins of different species. Hardly any protected their feet with skins tied with leather strips, most of the group went barefoot.

The buffaloes were a dangerous and fast prey, many times the hunter became the victim, for that reason they advanced with prudence, waving the torches and blocking the escape of the animal that undertook a crazy race towards the interior of the gorge looking for another exit in the rocky wall. When the hunters narrowed the semicircle, everything indicated that the animal would blindly throw itself into the void; they exchanged optimistic glances, tasting the prey beforehand.

It was at that moment that the buffalo did something unexpected.

In a quick movement he turned round, striking the nearest individual.

Enitarzi, a robust warrior in his thirties, tried to repel the animal with his spear, barely dodging the deadly horns that cut the air a short distance from his body. When going back one step the hunter stumbled on a rock, losing his balance, the buffalo went mad, delivering a strong blow to the hunter's leg. Arnut moved like lightning, thrusting into the animal's flank, preventing his fallen companion from being trampled. The spear broke as the furious animal turned to one side, feeling wounded. Several warriors stepped forward, waving their flaming torches, improvising a wall of lances around their fellow men in danger. Harassed by several dogs, wounded and frightened by the fire, the buffalo turned again to run blindly toward the gorge, until it rushed into the void. A deaf boom announced that the hunt was over, when the animal hit the stones about ten meters below. The group went down the ravine, it was necessary to protect immediately the place where the animal was dying. A warrior ended the suffering of the prey with a spear strike, while the rest of the group lit a couple of bonfires with the intention of rejecting the inevitable attack of hyenas and other scavengers, who would soon be attracted by the smell of blood.

The warriors gathered around the beaten animal. Some of them put aside the heavy spears used in the hunt, the most effective weapon against large animals, and now wielded bows, arrows and slight assegai that they could throw at a good distance using bone spear-thrower. Standing, they stood around the beaten animal, waiting, attentive. Half an hour later a group of women, children and old men arrived at the place; they had remained watching the hunt from a prudent distance. They carried water in the shells of ostrich eggs and animal bladders; the precious liquid was distributed among the group of hunters. The wounded man had his leg washed, before receiving a plaster of herbs to contain the bleeding. Fortunately, he didn't seem to have broken any bones, he would be able to return with the clan to the cave, leaning on his spear to walk.

After quenching the thirst, the group began the work: the buffalo was skinned; its thick skin, horns, tendons and helmets were removed. Large pieces of meat were cut, salted and arranged on long poles for transport. The viscera, kidneys and liver were roasted by the elders; that would feed the clan that day.

The heart was carefully reserved.

Smaller pieces of meat were arranged to dry in the sun, seasoned with salt and herbs. The children drove out some marauders with their bows and arrows, or simply throwing stones, while the dogs grunted threateningly.

It was dusk when they finished the work, at night they camped right there, at the base of the rocky wall, sheltered by large bonfires, fed with the abundant dry wood of dead vegetation.

The next day, the clan, transporting the product of the hunt, undertook the march. For two days they marched along the ancient dry bed of a great river, now transformed into an insignificant stream of water coming from the southern mountains, running swiftly to disappear into the subsoil of the semi-arid prairie, a few hundred kilometres further on. Sometimes, women would stop for a few minutes to collect some seeds, leaves or roots. On the morning of the third day they entered a small valley surrounded by a high plateau, the group walked for three hours towards the great stone wall at the other end of the valley, a faint column of smoke revealing human presence. At the base of the plateau was the entrance to a cavern, barely visible from a short distance, denounced only by the smoke rising from within. In the wide entrance, a couple of old people kept two bonfires burning, protecting the home from the attack of the big cats.

A huge dog of fierce appearance accompanied the sentries.

The animal did not bark at the group's arrival, as soon as it wagged its tail, warning the guards. The hunters emerged shortly after on the crest of a gentle hill, and the dog stepped forward to sniff out the arriving dogs. The cavern was wide, forming a vault about ten meters high in a kind of main hall, which was shrinking in size towards the bottom, to end in a series of small tunnels, which were used as deposits of old skins, bones, firewood, etc... In the central space were raised several wooden circular huts, solid, with a roof of branches, leaves and dry mud, all had beds built with thick branches that rose from the floor about 50 cm. They were covered with mattresses of leaves and skins.

In one corner a support of long rods was raised, used to store the fish and salted meat reserves. Shortly after the women added there the cuts of meat supplied by the group, Arnut could feel satisfied, because the reserve would feed the clan for a long time.

The cavern wall exhibited numerous cave paintings with hunting scenes, some from time immemorial, created by people that once occupied the place. Arnut's clan had also left their mark, painting animal figures during ceremonies of thanksgiving to the Gods. By the entrance they stored huge piles of firewood and sticks, sheltered from the inclemency of the weather.

The cave clan enjoyed a privileged location, a stream that was born on the plateau and ran about twenty meters from the cave, provided an abundant supply of water and, hopefully, some fish from time to time.

A day's march south could reach the sea, the main source of fish, crustaceans, birds and the important salt. The sea also facilitated communication with neighboring villages with which they exchanged food, furs and stone tools.

Comprised of a little over thirty individuals, the Arnut clan was more numerous than usual in those difficult times, rarely exceeding twenty members. Very high infant mortality rates and harsh adulthood limited population growth. People, with rare exceptions, were no older than 40.

Work concentrated entirely on survival, activities ranging from searching for food by hunting, collecting fruits, herbs or roots, collecting honey, or fishing; to making weapons, tools of carved stone, bones or carved ivory, wooden objects, making baskets of reeds and braided stems. It still took millennia for ceramics to be invented, the containers were improvised with turtle shells, ostrich eggs or large snails and seashells, which allowed them to transport water, store honey and ferment grains.

The whole group had to work; there was no place for idleness.

The elders took care of the fire, taught the hunting and fishing techniques to the children, who helped by gathering firewood, or collaborating with the women in the collection of seeds, fruits and roots. Wounded or incapacitated hunters repaired and manufactured weapons, modeling flint, obsidian, quartz or other hard and resistant minerals, to make scrapers, arrowheads and spears, axes, knives, sickles to collect wild seeds, etc. With bones they made harpoons and hooks, necklaces and ornaments. Adult men hunted, built huts, canoes, and defended the group, which was usually led by an old man respected by the entire clan for his experience and wisdom.

Akrabuamelu Arnut could be considered longevity, having reached the advanced age of 42 years. He had wisely led the group for many years after his father's death.

In spite of the scarce rains and the increasing aridity of the territory, during the last seven years, the clan did not need to emigrate, it had remained in that cavern benefited by the central position of the cavern, which dominated a wide virgin territory, mostly uninhabited, having as only neighbors the clans of the marine coasts. That contributed for the increase of the number of members, without needing to fight for its food, Arnut maintained good relations with the villages of the coast and some nomadic clans that very rarely appeared by the region. They exchanged skins, salt, horns, ivory, necklaces, ornaments, herbs, fruits, stones and meat. The mountainous region was also rich in gold, a mineral easy to mold, that the clan had learned to mold in cold to make small adornments that they commercialized with neighboring towns, it was the first steps in direction to the metallurgy, that millennia later would change forever the life of the Man, with the diffusion of the use of the copper.

It was the time of the year in which the clan celebrated the ceremony of gratitude to the Goddess Earth, dedicating him a buffalo or another animal of good size that had been the cause of the recent expedition of hunting.

The buffalo that was brought down days ago would have its head and heart offered to the Goddess.

It was a solemn occasion for the clan, because the day after the ceremony, was performed the ritual of initiation of young warriors.

At dawn, just before sunrise, all the members of the clan gathered on the hill in front of the cave. The attention of the group was directed towards the place where the first solar rays would emerge. Arnut, wearing his leopard skin thong, reserved for ceremonies, remained standing, with the ceremonial dagger raised towards the horizon, waiting motionless. At his side, on top of a large flat stone that formed a huge table, they had carefully arranged the heart and head of the buffalo, properly washed and adorned with leaves and flowers. As the first ray of the Sun flashed, Arnut's arm moved skillfully, simulating the act of slitting the buffalo's head in honor of Mother Earth. To his left an old man uttered some ritual words with his eyes closed and both hands raised in the direction of the Sun, thanked Mother Earth who fed and cared for her children, sending them animals, fruits, fish and seeds generously every year. The heart was offered to the sacred flames of the bonfire, culminating the ceremony.

Much of the buffalo meat was roasted and consumed by clan members. On other occasions, visitors from neighboring clans had participated in the banquet, sharing the same rituals with the cave clan.

Shortly after the ceremony, Enitarzi, the hunter wounded during the recent hunting expedition, approached Arnut walking with difficulty.
-Arnut, to save my life you lost your best weapon - He stood, supported by a thick rod - accepts this spear, I have worked on it for a long time, I reserved it for a special occasion.
The chief observed with admiration the stupendous spear, made of an excellent straight and solid branch, but not too heavy. Its tip attracted attention because it was made of ivory, in which had been carved the figure of a scorpion, perfect in its wealth of details. Arnut weighed the spear with his right hand, smiling satisfied. He placed the weapon on the wall of the cavern, and placing his right hand on the hunter's shoulder, he muttered:
-I should save your life more often, Enitarzi, it's a magnificent spear, and I thank you!
The footsteps of several warriors entering the cave were heard again, a woman braiding a net screamed with a child running beside the fire, playing with a dog. Arnut nodded slightly, saluting the warrior who placed a good-sized fish on a board.
-Have you seen Hor?
The warrior pointed to the outside.
- I've seen him, he was walking with Enuttaui a moment ago, maybe he's getting ready for the ritual," he commented with a certain sarcasm, starting some laughs in the group.
The wounded warrior murmured with a malicious gesture.
- I think we will soon have new children running around here.
The chief shook his head, smiling.
-I hope so, too. Tomorrow he will finally be initiated as an adult hunter.
In the wide strip of low ground, bordering the stream, there was still abundant vegetation, there the clan used to collect leaves and seeds that sprouted naturally. It would still take millennia for someone to relate the humidity of the river to the fertility of the soil and try to sow seeds, but people already knew the advantages and benefits of wheat, flax, millet and barley.
Groups of women and children leaned over the wild plants to collect with their sickles the cereals that many generations past had learned to grind to obtain the precious flour.
Enuttaui slowly climbed the hill, where he could see Hor leaning over a rock, concentrating on a task that the girl could not define in the distance. She was a young woman of about sixteen; thin, white skin slightly tanned by life out in the open, her hair a deep black color, long, combed in two braids that fell on her shoulders. She wore a skillfully sewn skin forming a tube that covered his neck up to his knees; she walked with his bare feet.

A little higher up, in the small grassy meadow, occasionally dotted with rocks, palms and shrubs, Hor leaned on a rock to cut the piece of wood he carved with his knife. Little by little the shape of a buffalo was insinuated into the wood.
The boy interrupted his work for a moment, to observe a young man walking towards the cave, with his body completely covered with mud, carrying in his hands part of a large beehive from which the golden honey dripped. The mud had protected his body from the attack of the bees, which he possibly drove away using smoke. A couple of children chased the young collector, trying to steal some drops of honey.
Enuttaui arrived with the boy.
-What are you doing?
He showed the wooden figure - It's for your little brother Gen.
She seemed surprised - For my brother?

Hor smiled for a moment.

-Maybe so he won't steal my things again, days ago I caught him playing with my bow.

They both laughed, funny. At some distance, a little further down, a band of pink flamingos took flight from the edge of the creek, to get lost behind the treetops, about three hundred meters away. She lowered her eyes as she commented.

-I heard it said that you took too much risk during the hunt.

-It's not true; my father won't let me go ahead with the hunters. He's always protecting me, keeping me on his back, or with the elderly. He humiliates me in front of the others!

The girl sat on a stone. Hor approached her side; a new expression revealed that her thoughts were now different.

-After my initiation, I will finally be able to build our hut.

She watched the boy in silence, which meant that they would soon form a family, with their own hut. She faked worry by asking:

-Are you ready for trial, future warrior?

-It shouldn't be much, from what I've heard among the hunters.

She finally seemed to understand the meaning of Hor's words:

-You said you will build our hut; shouldn't you consult my opinion first?

Hor laughed amusingly.

- I didn't know if you would accept!

-You're an idiot, a frog and fly hunter! You know I want it more than anything.

They hugged, remaining silent for several minutes.

The romantic moment was abruptly interrupted when a ball of mud crashed into Hor's back.

Back there, among the branches of a bush, was Gen, Menuttaui's little brother.

-Damn boy, he always spies on us!

Hor threw a stone at him and the boy ran down towards the cave, shouting provocative cries interspersed with a loud laugh, a dog barking happily jumping behind the boy.

-I don't think I'll give him the wooden buffalo, he doesn't deserve it.

One of them chuckled, making an obscene gesture for her friend as she added some branches in a bonfire, where she roasted some pieces of meat, and the first drops of fat squeaked on contact with the embers.

That morning Akrabuamelu Arnut gave his son Hor a recently hunted antelope skin while the old priest murmured some magical words to get help from Mother Earth.

All the young people, when they reached a certain age, were subjected to the test that determined whether they would be considered suitable hunters to take their place as adults, or should wait another year as simple auxiliaries to the warriors. It was a test of courage, intelligence and dexterity; the young man had to cover himself with the skin of some animal, to approach in the meadow of some herbivore, arriving to the smallest possible distance, without being discovered. The young man did not receive any kind of instructions, there were no rules, he could use tricks, it was about revealing the ingenuity of future warriors. The adolescent had no obligation to hunt the animal that should be decided in the moment. Only the great hunters had managed, in their initiation, to get close enough to pull the tail of the animal... and to get safe from its reaction to feel humiliated. Hor suspected that it was a lie created to encourage young debutants. The test would be accompanied at a distance by the clan, who would judge his behavior. For Hor that meant a lot, as long as he was not considered an adult warrior, he could not build his own hut or constitute a family with Enuttaui. Accompanied at a distance by several people, the young man walked to a place where they usually grazed herbivores. Shortly before arriving at the place, he covered himself with the skin of the animal, keeping the head of the antelope above his own head.

The sun wasn't too strong that morning, but as it rose in the sky, the temperature under that skin would rise considerably.

Imitating the behavior of an animal, Hor stood on all fours, observing the meadow that opened up to his forehead.

There were no signs of antelopes, just two gazelles grazing at less than a thousand meters. In that uncomfortable position he began to move towards the centre of the meadow, which he reached about half an hour later. He remained motionless for over an hour, sweating profusely. He knew that he was being watched from afar, he imagined his father comfortably installed under the shade of a tree, drinking fresh water and studying his movements.

Another hour passed slowly, the sun was stronger, approaching noon.

With the heat it seemed that everything had been interrupted in the meadow, the breeze was no longer blowing. Some insects flew around his head, his back hurt and his knees seemed to burn on contact with the earth. He slowly incorporated his body to take a look around... nothing, not even an animal.

An hour later, thirsty, he decided to change places, approaching a small stream of water running across the meadow, before flowing into the nearby stream of the cave.

Hor considered on several occasions to stand up and simply walk to the place, discarding all precaution, he restrained himself because that would frighten the animals that could be found grazing in the vicinity. He remained in that uncomfortable position. He was sweating a lot; the skin looked like an oven inside which he was roasting his own body.

How could the clan warriors have endured such torture? For a moment he thought he had seen the figure of an animal grazing in the distance, near the creek. It was a fleeting image, possibly deceived or the animal disappeared from the visual field behind the vegetation.

He crawled in that direction.

He was finally less than 100 meters from the waterway when he heard a slight sound that he could not identify. It was as if something very light had moved some small stones gently. As he slowly raised his head a cold sweat ran down his spine. There, less than a hundred feet to his left, a magnificent cheetah lurked, and his body glued to the ground.

The feline had simply ignored him, concentrating on something ahead. Hor carefully turned his head to discover a gazelle grazing close to the water. The herbivore sensed the danger as he watched around, his short tail agitated, revealing the animal's tension. The gazelle's instinct warned her of the danger, but something left her confused.

The cheetah had slipped two meters closer to Hor, ignoring the supposed antelope to try to capture the gazelle, his favorite prey.

At that moment Hor understood: the gazelle had identified him, but his trail, mixed with the smell of the antelope, had confused the animal. The feline advanced half a meter imperceptibly, with all his muscles tense, his belly almost dragging on the ground. Hor knew that in a few seconds the cheetah would throw itself in a fast race, if he could get one meter closer, the gazelle would be lost.

Hor sighed deeply; there was no other way out.

Suddenly he stood, waving his arms, he shouted:

-Cheetah out! Heeeeaaaaw!

The gazelle must have been frightened, fleeing at once, Hor couldn't tell, because all his attention was directed to the cheetah. The feline got the biggest fright of his life, when that antelope suddenly turned into a human being, less than fifteen meters away. In an instant he forgot his prey, to escape as quickly as possible in the opposite direction.

Hor removed the skin from his head, completely soaked in sweat and walked with slow steps to the creek to drink and refresh his body. He stretched his legs, still numb, massaged his waist for a moment, and with his skin over his shoulder he slowly went towards the edge of the forest, about four hundred meters away, where the whole group had witnessed what had happened.

He had failed.

As he passed without stopping in front of the group, something caught his attention... his father's gaze was not one of reproach, on the contrary, he seemed to discover a certain reflex of approval in old Arnut. The group returned following the young man's footsteps, in silence.

Hor heard no comment as he entered the cool shadow of the cave, where Enuttaui awaited him visibly moved. He embraced her feeling embarrassed, within her there was only one thought: I have failed... I have failed.

AGGA, THE RED-HAIRED WARRIOR.

The robust hunter must not have been more than thirty years old, a long reddish hair covered part of his face, in which shone a pair of cunning blue eyes. A sparse beard sprouted from his dimly accentuated chin.

He bent down to examine closely the marks which revealed to him everything that had happened there a few days before. At his side, the group of twenty hunters was also going through the place where the buffalo had crashed after falling down the cliff. They immediately understood the strategy used during the hunt, one of them pointed to the top of the rocky wall, and the leader barely made a brief nod. They examined the place inch by inch, attentive to the marks left during the work of skinning and preparing the meat of the animal for transport. One of them discovered different footprints and warned:

-Dogs. There are several.

Those warriors called themselves "Clan of the Moon", however they were known by other peoples as Red-Haired Men.

They constituted a group of original characteristics, presenting very clear skin, blue, gray or green eyes, the color of their hair oscillated between red hair and blond; they had short stature, none surpassed the meter and sixty, but all were of heavy and robust constitution.

All this revealed that their ancestors had left Africa in very remote times, long enough for environmental conditions to slowly transform them over many generations; their skin had thinned, as had their hair. Their physical constitution had been shaped by the glacial periods.

Nothing in them was reminiscent of Homo Heidelbergensis, his direct ancestor. They carried no bows or propellers, their spears were long, heavy and solid, with wide stone tips, some of them carrying powerful masses of stone and bones. Their bodies were covered with scars, one of which bore a dreadful mark covering half of his face, a reminder of the claws of a large animal, possibly a bear, which ripped out his left eye. They were adorned with wolf teeth and necklaces of shells, snails and claws of animals, they did not possess dogs. All exhibited black vulture feathers or eagles adorning their heads and weapons. Some wore ochre ink on their faces, which gave them a fierce appearance that terrified their enemies. They wore skins of bears, buffaloes or other large animals. They spoke little, using a completely different language, often communicating barely with gestures. Agga, the leader, examined some remains of food found in the ashes of the fires. With a hoarse voice, he muttered:

-They are twice the fingers of my hands, many women.

Beside him, Susuda, a warrior with brown hair, with bones pierced in both ears, smiled briefly at the word "women", pointing to the south with his spear.

-There they went; there are few hunters, many women.

-Towards the mountains- commented Agga, beginning the march.

In silence the group followed in the footsteps of the hunters. Before leaving, a warrior found a bone among the remains of a bonfire shook the ashes with small blows and began to bite it until breaking it, to extract the nutritious marrow. The group moved in silence, vaguely, they walked without stopping until dusk, accompanying the clear trace left by Arnut's group.

From time to time, someone would tear off the branch of a bush to devour its leaves or some fruit, which he would not divide with anyone. That afternoon, when they were preparing to camp, they came across a wounded impala, he had a fractured anterior leg, and marks of wounds produced by claws in his back. Possibly he had managed to escape the attack of some feline a few hours earlier, and had taken refuge among the branches of a bush. Before seeing him, the warriors had already smelled the fresh blood of the animal, which could not stand. Silently, the hunters formed a semicircle keeping a prudent distance from the mortal horns of the impala. They all attacked at the same time, striking hard with their spears, without throwing them. Red-Haired hunters usually sought the body to body, relying on their own weight and muscle strength, they supported the weight of their robust bodies on the spear to give firm and deep thrusts. The animal was shot down quickly.

They lit a small bonfire in a hollow, trying to hide the light of the night fire and not provoke too much smoke, which could alert possible enemies. Organized, they kept a sentry on top of a tree.

They used only salt to season the animal's flesh, and fed silently. The surplus meat was tied up on a long staff to be carried between two men. Shortly before dawn they set out, accompanying the footprints which they easily distinguished despite the dim light.

They walked the whole day, feeding without stopping, on the meat of the impala.

It was getting dark when they saw the light of bonfires from a distance, shining at the foot of a plateau. That night they did not camp, in silence they went towards the point of light.

They marched the whole night.

When they were about three kilometers from their target, reaching the top of a hill, the group stopped. Soon it would be dawn.

From that place the entrance to the cavern and its surroundings could be seen perfectly.

Agga placed his spear on the ground, looking for a comfortable position he sat down leaning an arm on a great rock. No one spoke a word; they were distributed around the leader, ready to wait patiently. They were getting ready to sleep, with a gesture Agga indicated to one of his warriors that he should remain on guard. Without saying a word the man made a brief movement with his head, back several meters down the slope to a rock, below which opened a small cave. Lying face down on the ground, he examined the cavity for a few minutes, inserting his spear. Shortly after he joined the group, in his hands he carried the body of a lizard that began to skin. Some of his companions were already asleep.

He had hunted his breakfast, preferred to mount guard of full belly, because the wait could be prolonged. Comfortably seated behind a rock, he began to devour his prey chewing slowly, without diverting his attention from the cave.

MASSACRE IN THE CAVE

That morning Arnut seemed to be very worried when he sent his son Hor in search of his favorite dog, who had apparently left the cave overnight to run after a jackal and had not yet returned.

Hor walked the prairie to the stream, calling the dog from time to time. No one had said anything about his failure in the test the day before, which seemed rather strange to him. Menuttaui barely tried to console him, downplaying the matter. Inside it was repeated over and over again that he had been an idiot in wanting to save a gazelle, ruining the chance of being considered an adult. Now he would have to wait several months for a new chance.

After an hour of unsuccessful search, the young man returned to the cave, next to the entrance and his father awaits him. When Hor began to explain that he found no sign of the dog, the animal emerged from inside the cavern and passed by him, running after a small rodent that disappeared among the stones.

Demonstrating surprise, he pointed at the animal.

-He returned alone? Where was that bandit hiding?

Arnut did not answer him, he placed an arm on the shoulder of his son, leading him towards the interior of the cavern, and several people were in front of a small hut that Hor had not seen before.

He assumed that it should have been built the night before. Hor gave him only an indifferent glance, perceiving it to be an unfinished construction; he still needed many details to be inhabited.

His father Arnut, Serqui, Menuttaui's father and the young woman's mother, Inkaunaui, as well as several curious people, had gathered in front of the cabin. Everyone seemed to be having fun with that situation, judging by his expressions; however the boy felt confused, something bothered him but he did not know well what it was.

-What's going on here?

His father adopted an attitude that he pretended to be solemn, arms folded.

-My son, we reserve this surprise for you, to celebrate your initiation as a clan warrior.

Surprised, Hor babbled.

- Initiation? I thought I had failed, that cheetah ruined everything.

-I think you misunderstood everything, my son; this is not a hunter's trial.

Menuttaui stood beside her; she too seemed to be amusing herself with Hor's confusion.

- By placing the salvation of the gazelle above your own interest, you demonstrated the power of your heart, willing to sacrifice for others, setting aside personal interest. We are not interested in warriors without initiative, who barely follow their hunting instinct.

-I thought the clan preferred to have good hunters.

-We already have the best hunters, but the group needs first of all a good leader, who demonstrates not only courage but also a good heart.

Menuttaui's father, smiling, completed.

-We have all concluded that yours was an attitude worthy of a future leader.

-Then why didn't you say so yesterday when we returned to the cave?

Menuttaui intervened, taking him by the arm.

-We needed to buy time to build the cabin before talking to you.

-This hut was built for me...for us?
-We raised it during the night, but you will have to finish it.
He looked back at the girl.
-You too were part of this?
-My father told me last night, but they forbade me to reveal it to you.
Now everyone laughed and had fun with the expression of the young man, who examined the hut.
-Then can we occupy our home?
Arnut held him by the arm.
- Calm down, not yet, young man. Tomorrow we'll go hunting; you need new skins for your marriage bed.
-You still have a lot to do to live in that hut or do you think we'll do everything for you- exclaimed a warrior in the background.
Hor and Menuttaui exchanged a funny look, but Inkaunaui took his daughter by the arm to lead her outside the cave, where other women were already doing their daily work.
-Come on, work awaits us!
In an instant the group dissolved.
When everyone had left, little Gen emerged from his hiding place under the bed, next to him, his inseparable dog wagging its tail, the boy's gaze shining, as the new cabin had been at the disposal of both for the rest of the day, which promised to be a lot of fun.
-Do you have enough arrows for tomorrow?
Hor understood that it wasn't a question, his father was ordering him to prepare for the hunt, and he didn't need to answer. He went to the corner of the cave where they deposited the flint reserves, carrying several stones, the boy sat down on a dry trunk to begin the work of lascar and mold the arrow tips.
A little further on, a teenager was cleaning a large sea turtle shell, which would be used as a container for cooking food, protected by a layer of dry mud. A technique those centuries later would lead to ceramics.
Hor prepared a dozen arrows, dedicating a good part of the afternoon to make several light lances, which thrown with propellers can reach up to fifty meters, causing deadly injuries. The young man was not very addicted to the bow, he preferred lances. He had already witnessed some animals survive and escape despite being hit by two or three arrows.
At nightfall, the women prepared food after an old man separated a good number of embers from the large bonfire at the entrance.
Several pieces of succulent meat from different animals were arranged on stakes. Someone approached with a couple of fish that, strung on sticks, were placed next to the others, forming a semicircle in front of the embers.

Each family contributed with what they had, although the food would be consumed by the whole clan, without any kind of distinction. Four enormous dogs waited seated, a short distance from the fire.

In one corner, the women piled up a dozen ostrich egg shells containing water. Little by little, the darkness increased on the outside of the cavern, illuminated by the two bonfires. Occasionally someone caught a flying insect, which approached attracted by the light of the fire. The insects made a tasty mouthful, while the meats roasted slowly, releasing a pleasant aroma that flooded the interior of the cavern.

Everyone had fun disputing flying insects, when someone hunted a nocturnal butterfly; he celebrated by savoring it with exaggeratedly victorious gestures. The butterfly was considered, among the nocturnal flying insects, as the most appetizing delicacy.

Sometimes a teenager threw a small stone with some leaves arranged to give form of insect, the group amused itself when witnessing that someone was deceived, jumping to catch it to the flight. On occasions when most of the men were absent, children and women would engage in combat with pebbles or balls of mud, running cheerfully through the cavern in the middle of the night, completely safe under the protection of bonfires, dogs, and some old man standing guard at the entrance.

The sentry was responsible for keeping the fire burning throughout the night. For the women and children of the clan, those hours were the most pleasant of the day.

At dawn the group of ten hunters left, taking with them most of the dogs. The day before Arnut had been informed of the presence of a small herd of different species of herbivores of good size, grazing on the edges of the desert, two days' march north. It was a good place for a hunt, there they had captured good prey on previous occasions, and Arnut did not think twice, ordering the departure immediately.

The group carried a handful of torches, which at the appropriate time would be lit to scare and lead the animals to a ravine at the bottom of a short gorge between the steep walls of the hills. If the fence worked, they could capture a good number of animals, which meant abundant food for the clan for a long time, as well as skins, horns, tendons, etc., and skins for their son's new hut.

Arnut preferred to leave the ivory spear in the cave, choosing another with a hard flint tip, more resistant than ivory.

In the cave remained women, children, some elderly, and Enitarzi, the hunter wounded in the leg. The young Menuttaui planned to work the whole day in the hut destined for her future home, intertwining reeds and some branches with which she would make a protective curtain against insects, which would be installed in the door of the hut. On the bed, wild cow leather, belonging to his mother, had been placed on a thick cover of leaves. The young woman trusted that Hor would return with good skins, because that bed did not seem to be very comfortable.

Menuttaui smiled, wrapped in her thoughts, glancing tenderly at the bed. Her hands moved skillfully braiding the flexible stems, demonstrating mastery of a very ancient technique, transmitted by her mother during her childhood. Little Gen rushed into the hut with a huge lobster in his hand, swiftly passing his sister's side, to hide under the bed. Before the girl began to protest, the dog jumped out of a leap into the boy, who screamed amusingly. With the lobster in its snout, the animal left the cabin, while Menuttaui hit the boy several times with a bunch of sticks. Gen left the cabin calling the dog. A mature woman, who was grinding wheat grains on a stone pylon, smiled as she watched the boy run tirelessly after his faithful friend.

The animal had already lay down next to the fire and was about to devour the lobster, when Gen held it by the hind legs to drag it back, the dog roared furiously, but the boy ignored his apparent fury, letting out a roaring laughter. Gen picked up the lobster from the ground, and with the trophy in his hand he ran to the bottom of the cavern, the dog followed him, barking.

The old man taking care of the fire had fun watching the dispute between the boy and his friend. A few meters further back, Enitarzi, still with his leg quite swollen, covered with medicinal herbs, was preparing arrows. From time to time he proudly gazed at a flint dagger he made that morning. At his side rested a bow, which he would later use to test the effectiveness of the new arrows. To do so, he waited for little Gen, or some other child, to approach him to help him.

He needed to place a trunk, lined with a skin, at a certain distance, in order to use it as a target.

While no one approached, he continued to cut stones by striking small blows on a piece of flint. At each stroke, sharp flakes fell off, and he examined them carefully. The best were selected, being piled up to one side.

In his cabin, Serqui gave the final touches to a gazelle skin with its flint scraper. Sitting next to the entrance, he occasionally stopped to gaze smilingly at the mischief of his son Gen. That boy promised one day to be a great warrior, he said to himself mentally with pride. Enitarzi seemed to guess his thoughts, because he shouted at him:

-What do you feed him? That boy never stops, he's tireless!

-It's true, he runs the whole day, just seeing him makes me feel older.

From the hill, about two kilometers away, Agga and his warriors kept their eyes open. They had witnessed the group of hunters leaving the cavern at dawn. Without moving, they carefully accompanied the march of the warriors and their dogs until they disappeared in the distance.

It was the expected opportunity; they calculated that only women, old people and children should remain in the cavern. With a brief gesture from the leader, the twenty warriors set themselves in motion. In complete silence, they approached the cavern marching down a hollow. At all times they took into account the direction of the wind, so as not to be discovered by the dogs.
With barely two hundred meters to go, they gathered behind the hill that dominated the entrance to the cavern. Agga carefully peered her head through the sparse vegetation, scrutinizing the opening, from which emanated a white column of smoke.
Apparently there was no one outside, he slowly observed the surroundings, and everything seemed to be calm in the meadow up to the little forest in the background. In front of him, only the small stream stood between his group and the entrance to the cave, which represented no obstacle, the path ran down a gentle slope that descended to the rocky wall.
With a brief gesture, he ordered Susuda, his best warrior, to approach the base of the rocky wall. With a short detour, Susuda arrived crawling cautiously less than a hundred yards from the cavern. Suddenly he rose to his feet, and walked at a fast pace, avoiding running, until he reached the wall. On the hill Agga waited for a reaction from inside the cave. Everything remained calm; no one had noticed Susuda's approach, which crept in less than two meters from the entrance.
He glanced towards the place where his companions were waiting.
It was time to attack, Agga abandoned all caution and advanced with a fast pace straight to the cavern, followed by the whole group.
At the entrance, the dog beside the campfire threw a dry bark, the old man looked at the hairs on the animal's back raised, in a clear sign of alarm. As he looked out he saw the group of armed warriors walking in their direction. The old man shouted loudly, pointing his hand at the intruders.
At the sound of the alarm Serqui and another old man came out of their cabins to run towards the entrance, one of them lifted a heavy club. The old sentry wielded his spear, waiting at the entrance, when suddenly Susuda emerged to his right. Surprised, the old man did not react in time, the enemy's spear pierced him at the waist. The dog jumped over the aggressor, who defended himself with his forearm, as he pulled out the spear from the old man's fallen body.
At that height Agga's group was already invading the cavern, the woman who was grinding wheat ran giving the alarm, and several faces appeared in the huts.
From her corner, Enitarzi prepared the bow, trying to straighten her body, ignoring the pain of the wounded leg. Agga made a quick gesture towards the warrior, two men with red hair headed towards the wounded man.
At that moment Susuda managed to stick his spear in the dog.

Enitarzi shot the first arrow that sank in the belly of his enemy, the individual stopped to collapse with a gesture of pain. However it was too late to shoot another arrow, the spear of the second warrior pierced his chest.
Mortally wounded, Enitarzi still tried to grab the dagger, when a second thrust hit him in the throat. A little farther back Serqui received a heavy blow to the head falling senselessly, from his head gush abundant blood.
The other old man was also shot down by an accurate spear strike.
The invaders ran towards the huts, leaving in their wake the inert bodies of their victims, some women screamed as they were captured by the intruders. An invading warrior was placed at the entrance of the cavern to prevent the escape of any survivor.
It was a fast and implacable attack, in a few minutes all the men, their dogs and some children lay motionless; the women however were not wounded, they tied them with vegetable fibers and strips of leather.
In his cabin Menuttaui had heard the cries of alarm and pain; from the door she witnessed in horror those individuals invading the cave after murdering the old guardian. Desperate, she searched eagerly for something she could use as a weapon, barely having a thick branch that she tried to pull from the base of the bed. She was leaning against the bed when an enormous hand held her by her hair and dragged her outward.
The cries of the wounded and the crying of the women were heard everywhere. The intruders seized the meat reserves, some stone tools, skins, ivory ornaments, small necklaces of gold figures and snails. They destroyed everything that did not interest them, at the bottom of the cave they found the grain reserve deposited in large sea turtle shells and several tanned skins. Judging by their cries of joy, they seemed to attach great importance to the salt they found stored in reed baskets.
Coming out of a hut, Agga proudly displayed Chief Arnut's spear, with its carved ivory tip. The warriors threw firewood into each cabin, in a few minutes the fire spread throughout the place, a black smoke filled the cavern making it difficult to breathe. Loaded with plundered booty, the warriors led the eight captive women outside. Susuda had covered her shoulders with the large leopard skin that Arnut wore during religious ceremonies; smiling, the redheaded warrior displayed himself in front of his companions, who praised his trophy.
In a small chamber at the bottom of the cavern, hidden among the stones, the little Gen held his dog's snout tightly, avoiding his barking.
He had managed to go unnoticed.
The victorious looters gathered on the prairie in front of the cavern, Agga examined his warriors and the group of captives with satisfaction. It had been a great victory, for he had barely lost a man. With a gesture, the leader selected two men to transport the dead comrade's body.
The group began the march, leaving the place.

They formed a silent column, where the women's muted sobs were barely heard. With his arms tied to a rope that connected him to the woman walking to his forehead, Menuttaui turned his head to contemplate for the last time the entrance to his home.

After verifying that the attackers had left, Gen went through the interior of the cave looking for his parents in anguish. Finally he found Serqui, who seemed to have a serious wound on his head, where he was bleeding copiously. With great effort, the boy helped his father, who crawled outwards. He reached for water with a handful of leaves that he dipped in the stream. The man seemed to recover for a moment, without rising he looked around, his expression terrified. Holding the boy by the arm, he spoke choppily.

-Listen, you must look for the hunters, there is no time to waste, and they took your mother and sister. Take the dog and don't waste time, always walk north, you understand? To the north- he pointed his hand in that direction. -The dog will help you, go! Run!

Frightened, little Gen left the cave running, to go directly in the direction indicated by his father. He drank water from the stream; he had nothing with which to transport the precious liquid.

He set out, followed by the dog, into that wild meadow where adults would never allow him to venture.

It was a terrible day for little Gen, that afternoon the dog defended him from the attack of a lonely hyena wandering the vast plain. The hungry animal followed them at a distance for hours, but the fierce resistance of the dog finally made him give up the prey.

The relentless desert sun punished Gen, who nevertheless walked all day long. He was already faint when the sun disappeared on the horizon, relieving his suffering. The dog barked as he sniffed the proximity of water, in a few minutes led him to a well containing a scarce liquid of a brown coloration, in the cracked bed of a dry river. They both drank, quenching their thirst momentarily. The boy rested for a few minutes and stood up to continue the march tenaciously, he was on the edge of his strength, but he knew it would be better to march during the night, avoiding the sun and high daytime temperatures.

He marched all night without stopping, and found only a couple of gazelles that undertook a swift escape as they approached, but fortunately there were no signs of carnivores. Near dawn, Gen fell faint among some rocks, looking for a minimum of protection against the possible attack of some carnivore; there he would have some shade to escape from the sun that in a few hours would go to burn the meadow. The faithful dog remained by his side in a vigilant attitude, with his entire senses alert, even though he had lay down next to the rock and seemed to sleep. The slightest sound alerted their fine ears, though fortunately nothing happened during the hours they rested.

The child slept soundly most of the morning.
The sun was already high when he woke up, all the muscles of his small childish body hurt and his stomach demanded food.
Tortured by thirst, he walked slowly, always keeping the morning sun on his right, as he had been taught, the dog followed him at a short distance, sometimes going forward exploring the terrain, to wait for the child, who staggered and with short steps, struggled to maintain the march. When he felt faint, the memory of the massacre and the image of his mother and sister being taken captive made him gather strength to move forward. Above his infant head, the sun punished implacably, with his eyes closed, he was still walking, but without maintaining the direction, the dog was barely serving as a guide when he came forward and barked at him, calling his attention.
Twice he fell, remaining seated on the hot sand, and on both occasions the dog came, waving at his side, shaking his face until he saw it rise and restart the march. On the second occasion, the animal bit his arm to make it react.
He should not fall asleep, if he did he would be lost, he would never wake up under the sun of that clean sky, eternally without clouds.
Finally, a little after noon the dog barked several times running ahead, this time his barks were different, he was more agitated, but the child had no strength to follow him and let himself fall, had reached the limit of his strength.

Arnut and his hunters found themselves erecting a palisade to reinforce the natural fence where they planned to capture the flock the next day, when a sudden bark surprised them. Hor immediately recognized the dog that ran in his direction. Everyone watched the field around; apparently there was no one in sight.
Hor had bowed to caress the head of the agitated animal.
-Did he come alone?
-It's not possible that he followed us, something happened!
Barking, the dog caught the attention of the group, starting a short race to the place where Gen was, all of them came.
Immediately the hunters examined the boy, moistened his head and offered him water, which Gen drank avidly.
Shortly afterwards, the boy related briefly what had happened, before fainting.
The cacique left the hunt immediately, gathering the group dispatched several explorers to the main known trails, trying to find traces of the attackers, at the same time sent his son Hor with two warriors back to the cave, to help potential survivors and regain control of the local. Little Gen would be carried alternately by the two men, who carried him on their backs, tying the boy's hands around his neck. In this precarious position, Gen slept most of the day.

The journey that the boy took a day and a half to complete was covered in just one day by the three hunters, who did not stop at any time nor did they feed themselves, they only quenched their thirst during the march.
Several hours after dusk they reached the cave, everything was silent.
The bonfire was slowly extinguishing.
Lying next to the fire, on an improvised bed of branches and some remains of skins, Serqui, Gen's father, seemed to sleep soundly, his body was shaken from time to time by slight spasms, Hor had to shake it hard to make the man wake up, his forehead was covered by a crust of dried blood. One of the warriors offered him a snail shell with water, which the man drank avidly.
-Where is my son? Gen, Gen! - The old man tried to stand up but Hor's steady hand stopped him.
- Calm down, Gen is fine, he's just tired, he found us yesterday- he pointed his head at the place where the sleeping child had been placed, on an improvised mattress of leaves, branches and partially burned skins. The men had lit torches and after examining the cavern for a few minutes, returned to the entrance, Hor interrogated them with his gaze, without saying a word, both shook their heads indicating that there were no survivors.
Serqui muttered, holding him by the arm.
-They took all the women, Inkaunaui and little Menuttaui.
Hor tightened his jaw, feeling helpless. He could do nothing until he received news from his father; he trusted that the group would be able to intercept the looters.
He examined a broken spear, abandoned by the enemy.
- The men of Red Hair, those damned! -
He threw the spear into the fire with a furious gesture.
After burying the corpses deep in the cavern, following the ancient rites of the clan, they cleaned the place, removed the charred remains from the huts, collected enough firewood for the night, and lit a second bonfire at the entrance.
They fed on the last remnants of dried meat, there was nothing else they could do, just rest during the night to regain strength.
A lot of work awaited them for the next few days.
Hor barely managed to sleep for brief intervals, tortured by anxiety and a sense of helplessness. At all times he imagined Menuttaui in the power of those savages and a feeling of hatred and despair kept him tense.
Shortly before dawn Hor rose and approached the campfire at the entrance to the cavern, where Serkes, one of the warriors, slept, immediately awoke to hear the young man's footsteps.
-Go rest, Serkes, I'll stand guard.

The warrior simply stepped aside, placing his body on the ground, and in a few seconds he slept soundly. Hor placed some trunks on the fire and sat a short distance away, looking at the silhouette of the trees, drawn by the moonlight.
All was silent in the meadow. A whirlwind of thoughts flooded him, his world had been destroyed. The burnt remains of the huts and the absence of so many familiar and beloved faces tortured him, he thought continuously of Menuttaui. Among the tops of the trees, drawn in the distance under the first lights of dawn, he seemed to see the face of the girl, calling anguished.

Far from the cave, in the middle of the night, Agga suddenly interrupted the march.
Without saying a word, he examined the place carefully, his men stopped by his side, looking closely at the terrain around him. The light of the full moon allowed them to see the details; the mighty river descended from the distant mountains to run fast to the north, a few miles ahead it described a steep curve. The place where the group had stopped was the only point where the current could be crossed with some safety. His experience as a warrior told him that this was the perfect place for an ambush. In stark contrast to the arid meadow, the place was covered by thick vegetation and rocks from which they could easily dominate anyone who dared to cross the river.
Agga knew he had left behind a strong group of at least ten well-armed veteran warriors accompanied by dogs. That group would soon return to the cave and discover what was happening. He tried to guess what the leader of that clan would do... follow them? Or remain inactive just regretting the disaster, perhaps he would simply decide to emigrate to other lands? He turned to his trusted man.
-What would you do in the place of the enemy chief, Susuda?
-I would try to recover the women- was the laconic response of the warrior, who chewed on a long stalk of grass.
-Perhaps they do not know that the women are in our power; they did not find their bodies in the cave but they can suppose that they fled to another place.
Susuda smiled slightly.
-They will come, Agga, they know the women were captured.
Agga reflected for a brief moment, glancing around.
-I know, I would do the same... yes, they will come.
Agga always agreed with Susuda, in time that practical warrior had become her trustworthy man. During the critical moments of each combat, both understood each other with just one glance that was always decisive to emerge victorious from the most difficult situations.
-I don't like to leave living enemies behind me- he muttered with a slight smile - when they come, we will be waiting for them here.

No other words were necessary, they began to inspect the place in detail, the whole group had understood, some went away to cut logs with which they would make stakes, while some of them watched the captives, who waited on the banks of the river, drinking and trying to wash their wounds.
-Come on, get up quickly! Get up! - ordered a warrior, striking the women, who slowly obeyed, helping each other to stand up.
The river was not more than forty meters wide at that point, the group walked through it among rocks and sandbanks, without worrying about hiding their traces. Once on the opposite shore, they moved away to a hill, about four hundred meters away. There the group split up, most of the warriors described a wide detour, this time erasing their tracks, until they returned to the place of the ambush.
On the other side of the hill, after walking a thousand meters, the three remaining warriors stopped, improvising a camp without lighting a fire remained watching the captives that piled at the foot of some rocks. The women sat on the sand, trying to rest.
- What do you think is happening?" asked one of them to Inkaunaui, the oldest of the captives.
-I don't know, I think they're waiting for something.
Hearing the whispers, the nearest guard kicked the woman's back hard, and she let out a drowned lament of pain.
-Silence, try to sleep until dawn - from the looted cargo he extracted a strip of dried meat which he began to chew, without ever neglecting the captives.
The remaining sixteen warriors were distributed throughout the pass. Remains of some animals hunted during the day were placed among rocks and bushes; when their stench decomposed it would hide the trail of the ambushed warriors, confusing the smell of the dogs. Agga sent the fastest of his men to settle two kilometers further back. At the first sign of the enemy, he should run to alert the group.
They prepared to wait, with the patience that only true hunters have. During the waiting time, they fed without lighting fires, consuming raw meat, and perhaps some wild fruits available in the vicinity.
They spent the next day getting to know the place in detail, each of them knowing exactly where he should be placed for the ambush. Some rocks in the center of the current were an excellent position to attack the enemy at close range, nullifying the effectiveness of their bows and arrows. Agga ordered to install sharp stakes in certain places under the water; they would make difficult the movements during the crossing. Everything was ready, the patient hunters waited for the prey.
The only movement that denounced its presence during those days was the warrior who, every morning transported water for the captives and their

guardians. The rest of the group was invisible, they had become part of the landscape, in a few hours the fauna resumed its routine of feeding and singing among the vegetation, accustomed to the presence of intruders.
At dawn of the third day of waiting, Susuda heard the agitated breathing and the heavy steps of the man from the advanced position, who returned running.
The guy passed by him, crossing the river without stopping. Before reaching the opposite margin, even with the water at his waist, he gestured in the direction of Agga, showing both hands open.
-Attention, warriors, they are coming, there are ten- warned Agga, raising his voice for the first time, the guardian paused to drink in the river, before adding:
-They have three dogs.

Akrabuamelu Arnut was a prudent and wise chief, all his men were fully confident in their decisions, so no one opposed when the chief went to the river crossing without stopping to examine the place. The footprints were from several days ago and it seems that the looters were marching without taking any precaution, possibly thinking that they had killed all the inhabitants of the cave. Arnut and his men were furious and impatient to reach them and rescue the women, perhaps that's why they did not take precautions when they reached the river, they underestimated that cowardly enemy who enslaved women and killed old men.
Silently Arnut examined the footprints for a moment and entered the river, the group continued to face the strong current. They had just made a fatal mistake. The hunters walked slowly trying to avoid the unevenness in the river bed, some managed to jump a few meters from stone to stone, before entering the water. As they approached the center of the river, the more advanced ones moved with water up to their waist probing the bed with their lances.
 It was at that moment that one of them uttered a drowned exclamation of pain when he stumbled on a sharp stake placed under the surface; the blow produced a deep cut in his leg. Supported by his companions, the hunter was transported among the great rocks in the center of the river.
Arnut stood guard, who had placed those stakes? Were they there long ago or was it an ambush? Observing their chief examining the surroundings visibly alarmed, the warriors lifted their spears without stopping the march. In front of him, the crossing seemed to be easier, as the depth decreased. The dogs had remained in the margin, barking without deciding to enter the water, or had they detected something abnormal?
Arnut wasted no time in calling them; they had to get out of the water immediately. He knew that when the group met on the opposite side, the animals would jump into the water so as not to be left behind. All his attention was focused on the vegetation on the shore, if there was an enemy lurking, he would

attack when they were approaching the edge, vulnerable even in the water. Half of the group had already passed through where Agga was hidden; in the center of the river... it was time. He glanced fleetingly at the only warrior he could see from where he was. No order was necessary, the subject understood, he emerged from a jump from the rock where he was hiding and with a quick movement he lifted his stone nail to crash it with force into the head of the nearest warrior. The man fell silently forward, fulminated; his body sank into the water. His companion, who followed him two meters away, when witnessing the Red Hair warrior hitting his companion, lifted the spear, but the distance was too narrow to throw it on the enemy, he should fight body to body, he charged with his spear at the ready when Agga came to his right sinking his heavy spear into his side, uttered a loud cry of pain and leaned, seriously wounded, on the rock next to him. On his back the stone nail shone for a moment in the semi brightness of dawn, before falling violently on the head of his second victim. The man who was wounded in the leg was momentarily isolated from the rest of the group when his closest companions were knocked down, he could not walk without help, he leaned on a rock trying to defend himself, but he was quickly knocked down by a spear.

The fight became generalized in the agitated waters of the river; nobody had time to prepare their bow to defend themselves. Superior in number and fighting body to body, the robust Red-Haired Men had no difficulty in imposing themselves on the enemy group.

In full combat, Arnut suddenly came face to face with Agga, who lifted his spear in the direction of the enemy. Arnut recognized the familiar ivory tip of the spear that was now in the hands of the enemy that must have surprised him, because he hesitated for a fraction of a second. Without giving him time to react, Agga gave him a strong blow to the chest, Arnut opened his mouth enormously, but fell back in silence, and his body disappeared into the current accompanied by a large spot of blood that danced madly before diluting in the water.

Agga stopped triumphantly, contemplating the ivory tip with the figure of the bloody scorpion, had just killed the enemy chief with his own spear; an intense sense of power intoxicated him. From the margin, the dogs barked furiously, without entering the water, Susuda threw a stone to them with a derogatory gesture.

Everything happened very quickly, in less than five minutes the seven hunters had died, among them the clan chief. For their part, the looters had two casualties, caused by the last warriors of the column, who, favored by the distance, had time to prepare their bows and shoot their arrows at the enemies before being eliminated. Agga and his men barely looted three corpses lying between the rocks, because most of their victims were washed away by the current disappearing downstream. Immediately the victors, transporting the bodies of their two comrades fallen in combat, went to meet with the group that took care of the captive women. At the top of the hill, Agga launched a victorious roar surrounded by his men, raising his arms toward the sun that was already rising on the horizon.

-Warriors, this was only the beginning. Someday we will celebrate an even greater victory after defeating the peoples of the Great River!   The entire ecstatic group shouted the name of their leader; their strong war roar was repeated in multiple echoes over the hills -Agga...Agga!

The victorious leader raised in triumph the spear of the defeated chief, the ivory tip threw a silver flash when receiving the first rays of the sun.

HOR'S ODYSSEY

In the following days, Hor and his warriors dedicated themselves to reorganizing the cavern, built two huts, and a new meat reserve was stored after a quick hunt in the vicinity. The salt had been plundered, so it was necessary to dry the meat in the sun.
Hor and Serqui, recovered from their wounds, dedicated an entire day for the manufacture of arrows and spears. Even the little Gen worked intensely in those days, collecting fruits, herbs, gathering firewood or fishing in the stream.
With each passing day, concern grew in the group as they received no news from Arnut and his group.
On the fourth day, in the morning, the three dogs of Arnut's group suddenly returned to the cave. Hor examined them, noting that they were not wounded, barely exhausted and hungry.
-My father would never leave the dogs alone.
Serkes stroked the head of one of the animals.
-Something has happened.
-It's impossible that these animals have left the group to return- said Serki - something serious has happened, without doubts.
Hor decided to leave in search of the group led by his father.
-We can't wait any longer.
The next morning Hor left the cave, supplied with dried meat, a bladder full of water, armed with bow and arrows.
As he dismissed him, Serkes gave him his spear with a propellant.
-Carry my weapon, I know you prefer it to a bow, and you'll need it.
 The young man headed north, following the trail left by Agga's group after the looting. The scarcity of rain in the region had preserved the tracks; Hor had no difficulty in guessing the course that the looters and their captives took. At dusk he discovered new footprints that joined the previous trail.

He knew the region well and immediately understood that his father had followed the same trail a few days before. Resting only for brief intervals, Hor walked all day and much of the night, keeping an eye out for the possible presence of felines in the meadow. The next morning he went into an extensive semi-desert meadow, it was a flat and stony terrain alternated from time to time by small bushes, in the distance some antelopes tried to feed on the miserable vegetation.

The stony terrain made traces difficult, but the few traces he found left no doubt about the direction taken by both groups.

That night he camped in the meadow, without daring to light a fire, he had heard the roar of lions in the distance, but they did not represent an immediate threat. He slept a few hours, and resumed his march when it was still dark.

A couple of hours after restarting the journey, at dawn he saw the silhouette of vultures flying at a great distance, over the green snake of vegetation that indicated the course of a river. A sudden premonition caused him great anguish, he hastened the step.   As he approached the river, several vultures took flight. He stopped at the margin of what appeared to be a natural ford. Two hyenas, their noses bloody, fled at the presence of the intruder. It was at that moment that he discovered the body of a warrior that he immediately recognized, despite being partially torn apart by the predators.

He frantically went around the place, finding several objects, some blood stains, a broken spear, a piece of torn bear skin, a necklace of eagle claws and some snails, characteristic of enemy warriors. Everything indicated that a bloody battle was taking place there. There were no other corpses.

- Possibly they have been carried by the current,- he said to himself.

He understood what had happened, that place was ideal for an ambush, and judging by the footprints, the looters had arrived several days earlier at the place, that could only mean that...

-My father was surprised by those bastards!

On the opposite shore, he identified abundant signs of the looting group, accompanying the footprints to the hill; he identified women's footprints next to the heavier footprints of Agga's men.

Hor paused for a moment, reflecting on what he should do next, return to the cavern to communicate the river massacre and organize a rescue expedition, or leave directly behind the enemy, following in his footsteps.

He decided to continue the pursuit, thinking of the captives.

The river, after being born in the mountains, descended directly to the north, running fast. Shortly after the place of the ambush, the river described a very pronounced curve to run southwest towards the sea, many kilometers ahead. In the entire territory north of the river curve, the traveler would only find water at a distance of eight or ten days' journey east.

During the rest of the day Hor followed the clear trail left by the enemy group, which apparently was confident, as it had discarded any precaution.

-They no longer wait to be attacked- he said while drinking a sip of water-They feel safe, I will take care of returning the anxiety to them.

That night Hor slept on a large solitary tree in the semi-desert region. The next day, the young man observed that the landscape was becoming even more arid, the stony plain was being replaced by sand dunes alternated by a reddish earth, a true desert with no signs of vegetation. He had to manage the remaining water until he found a source. Some time ago in the cavern Hor had heard stories of the elders, who described the region that extends north as a place of abundant rains, with much hunting and dense vegetation; the elders commented that suddenly everything had changed, the rains ceased and the earth died. Hunger had forced its inhabitants to emigrate, then came the people of Red Hair, a hostile race that attacked its neighbors, seizing the hunting grounds, kidnapping women and stealing what might serve him in some way.

The elders claimed that the land of origin of their own people was far to the north, a rich territory from which they had been expelled by the Red-Haired Men at the time of their parents' grandparents.

In the past Hor ventured into that region to the high hills that marked the end of that plain in the east. After that, he would be in unknown territory.

-The footprints do not lie, if they can cross this desert, I can too.

His people had preferred to explore in another direction, towards the west where the territory of the lakes began, between the two seas. He knew that by going even further west, he would reach the swampy area of the Great River Delta, bordering the great northern sea.

He returned his thoughts to the east, supposing that after the great hills he would reach the land of the Red-Haired men, though in reality he ignored it.

Absorbed in his thoughts, Hor walked without observing the surroundings, as was customary for all hunters. When he neglected himself, he ended up making a serious mistake.

It was a mistake that could have cost him his life.

A brief roar suddenly brought him back to reality, he stopped.

There ahead, less than fifty meters away, a huge leopard stared at him, crouching on the branch of the only tree in the immediate vicinity. It would be impossible to hit an arrow on a leopard during its swift attack.

With slow movements Hor watched around, as he hung the spear on his back to grasp the bow. The only shelter was forty meters to his left; it was a huge lonely rock between the mean vegetation and the reddish earth. He walked slowly towards the place, seeing his prey deviate from its course, the leopard jumped from the tree to move slowly in its direction.

- He's going to attack me- thought the young man, racing quickly towards the rock as he prepared the bow and increased the tension of the rope. Turning his gaze he saw that the feline was running smoothly in his direction, saving energy, in the certainty that there was no shelter for his prey. Hor began to climb the rock, which had no more than three meters at its highest point; he understood that the leopard would reach him without much effort.

He crawled into a cavity in the stone, where he fitted his foot and managed to stand up to defend him. He placed the bow and an arrow on the rock to grasp the spear. The leopard reached the base of the rock, its eyes fixed on its prey. Hor hit the animal's claw hard as he tried to climb. The beast stopped a little lower than where the young man took refuge.

Roaring, the leopard made brief claws at the tip of the spear. Seeing that the feline focused all his attention on his weapon, he held the spear with his legs, keeping the tip directed toward the animal's muzzle. With his hands free, he prepared the bow. At the exact moment when a strong chop pulled the spear from his knees, Hor pointed his bow carefully. The sound of the spear falling to the ground caught the animal's attention for a fraction of a second. Then the arrow was fired. About three meters separated the young man from the leopard, it was impossible to miss at that short distance. The arrow was buried deep in the chest of the beast, which launched a loud roar, the pain enraged him, but the rod that protruded from his chest, when a second arrow hit him in the side, behind the back leg. As he felt the bite of those wands for the second time, the leopard, in a reflex movement, leapt to fall to the base of the rock, where he twisted in pain. Crazy and bloodthirsty, the beast turned to its prey, preparing to jump to the top of the rock. The third arrow was shot calmly, Hor calculated the vital point of the animal, in this occasion the obsidian tip crossed the heart of the beast, that with a spectacular jump collapsed, agonizing between violent spasms.

The young man quickly descended from the rock to finish off the animal with his spear.

He interrupted the march for the rest of the day, to dedicate himself to removing the skin of the leopard, a trophy coveted by all hunters, symbol of authority and power. He carried the feline's body to the scarce shade of the tree from which he had jumped shortly before to attack him, about a hundred meters away. In spite of knowing that it would be risky, he discarded the precautions, lighting a bonfire to roast part of the meat of the feline. He prepared the skin with an improvised flint scraper, and spread it in the sun for the rest of the day.

-It's not enough, but it will be enough to preserve the skin until I can prepare it properly.

The smell of the leopard would be enough to keep other carnivores away. After feeding, he climbed up the tree, settled in the best possible way on a thick branch, where he slept the rest of the afternoon. In the evening, with a brief refreshing breeze, he resumed his march, heading for the distant hills to the northeast.

Agga stopped the march at noon. They had reached a small spring surrounded by a dense grove. He was satisfied, they had left the desert behind, those hills that rose a short distance ahead marked the beginning of his clan's territory. All drank avidly, had walked for two days without rest, the captives were exhausted.
After quenching their thirst, the warriors placed the bodies of their comrades on a flat rock; the corpses were swollen, beginning to decompose. They cut thick branches to tie them in the shape of X. Quickly two platforms were raised using trunks and some rocks.
The corpses were carefully placed on a mattress of branches at the top, and piled dry branches and trunks at the base of each platform.
When the work was finished, Agga pointed to one of his men as responsible for the funeral, and with the rest of the group resumed the march towards the hills to the northeast.
The warrior wasted no time, quickly lit a bonfire, from which he removed, shortly after, flaming splinters which he threw on the wood piled at the base of each platform, which began to burn.
He sat some distance away, gazing at the fire; he should remain there until the flames completely consumed the corpses, preventing them from being devoured by the scavengers that abounded in the vicinity. A large column of smoke rose lazily into the blue sky.
Hor followed the trail on the prairie as he watched the thick, dark gray cloud ascend a few miles ahead.

The red-haired warrior, his body covered in gazelle skin, sat on a stone, gazing at the platforms where the bodies of his companions had been transformed into dark silhouettes charred by the flames. He had placed himself with his back to the wind, to escape the dense smoke and the strong smell of burnt flesh that came from the bonfire.
Hor remembered old stories in which the elders described the incredible smell of the Red-Haired men, for that reason he made a detour to approach the wind from the front. The smoke coming in his direction was no inconvenience as it was on a lower level across the hill. As he leaned out on the opposite side of the spring, he could see the warrior sitting in front of a large bonfire, some three hundred meters away. He assumed it was a single warrior, probably a sentry.
He approached slowly, hidden in the dense vegetation of the place. When he was less than a hundred meters away, one of the platforms collapsed raising a cloud of brilliant sparks; the warrior approached the pyre accumulating firewood around a dark bundle that Hor could not identify at a distance. The young man took advantage of the occasion by running fifty meters in a fast race. The warrior was with his back to the second platform, which was delayed in falling, when a sudden current of air revealed Hor's approach, with a quick movement turned to

face the intruder, but at that moment he noticed a terrible detail: his spear was on the stone where he had remained seated, about ten meters to his left.
That had been a grave mistake.
Guessing his intentions, Hor walked in his direction, with the bow taut and an arrow pointed at the warrior.
-Don't! -shouted the young man, the redhead examined him for a moment, smiling contemptuously; he could see that it was a single enemy, too young to pose a threat to a proud, scarred warrior.
It was his second mistake.
Despising his enemy, he walked towards his spear, but did not have time to run; the arrow hit him in the stomach, burying him deeply. He let out a dull grunt of pain; however he did not stop, and continued fast until he wielded the long spear to wield it against Hor, who was already preparing the bow with quick movements. Barely twenty meters separated the two men, the warrior received the second arrow in his chest and stopped with an expression of deep surprise, he remained standing, leaning on the spear that sunk its tip in the sand.
Hor wasted no time, approached several steps and shot again, the third arrow penetrated very close to the previous one, in full chest. A deaf groan escaped the warrior's mouth, who still tried to walk staggeringly in the direction of his aggressor. With a trembling movement he plucked an arrow from the body, blood immediately gushed out.
It took a fourth arrow to knock it down. Hor slowly approached the wounded man, who was groping trying to get up, shaken by strong tremors. He had no pity, that warrior was one of those who massacred his people; an accurate spear strike put an end to his suffering.
 In that instant the second platform crumbled with a dry roar, Hor took a few steps away, while a pile of embers and burning wood covered the warrior's body. After quenching his thirst, the young man supplied his bag with water, examined the trail of the group for a few minutes before restarting the march to the northeast.
The landscape after the hills was different, from the height Hor saw a wide valley, at the bottom of which the waters of an enormous lake shore. At a distance it was impossible to calculate its size; the vegetation seemed to be abundant on its margins, contrasting with the ochre coloration of the plain that extended to its front, revealing an arid territory tinged by trees and palms.
It was the territory of the Red-Haired Men; the solitary invader began to walk towards the lake.

THE CLAN OF THE DESPERATE

Far to the west, somewhere in the territory that would one day be known as Libya, the group of four hunters walked through arid terrain, looking for signs of an animal that could still be found in the vicinity of the last water wells. They marched along the stony dry bed of an ancient river, occasionally passing by a rachitic shrub that resisted disappearing.

The different shades of yellow and brown of the landscape were altered here and there by bushes covered with reddish dust raised by the wind that blew permanently from the interior of the continent. Those warriors were individuals with shiny black skin, with very short curly hair. They adorned their ears and hair with small bird bones, some exhibiting a long ostrich feather over their head. From each man's neck hung a colorful necklace, formed by snails, shells and pebbles of vivid colors to which they had opened small holes through which they introduced thin strips of leather. They were tall individuals, none less than one meter and eighty of stature, very thin and agile, covered with leopard skins, impalas or gazelles. Leather bracelets on the arms and ankles completed his attire. All were armed with small bows composed of bones and wood, which could shoot small arrows with bone tip or carved stone, with a striking red feather on the opposite end. Erihen, the leader of the group, in addition to the bow, carried a very short, light spear with a bone propeller.

The group had walked all morning, since dawn, along the old dry riverbed, but they were not tired. Two warriors carried sacks made from the ostrich's crop, in which they carried water.

Arriving at the lowest part of a hill, the leader stopped, reflected for a moment, to point to the right:

-It's been several days since we've covered the rocky meadow on that side.

Nobody said anything, they just changed course to go in the right direction. They walked the whole day, sometimes separating into two groups to cover a larger territory. At the end of the day, they returned to camp looking tired. All day long they had only hunted three small rodents and a lizard.

The miserable camp stood next to a rock wall, the limited space of a cavity in the rock had been augmented by a hut built of ancient mamuth bones, which abounded in the vicinity, as proof of the richness of that territory in times past. Some branches and a covering of skins completed the shelter. The high rock wall had paintings of hunters, buffaloes, lions, hyenas, wild horses and elephants, the eternal memory of happy times, the work of men who had long since left.

In the precarious shelter piled men, women and children, several of them sick, an old man had died that morning while the hunters were absent; his corpse was still lying in the shelter. A hunter lifted the inert body to transport it to the outside, depositing it under a bush, about twenty meters away. They would bury it later, if the hyenas did not devour it before. The water well adjacent to the shelter was drying; the hunters drank with anxiety a dirty liquid, of reddish brown color.

The clan's situation had become complicated after the first sandstorm, which surprised them at dawn two weeks ago. As a result, they lost two elders, one child and three women in the group.

Two years earlier, far to the south, in the interior of the continent, when they left their native land, the group was composed of members of three clans, a total of fifty individuals among warriors, women, children and elders who, punished by a terrible epidemic that did not spare animals or human beings, had united to escape from the valley, migrating northward, where the elders claimed that the climate had always been beneficial, and a great river fed the men.

During the nights, when the clan gathered around the bonfires, the elders told stories of a land protected by the gods, a land where all were welcome. Carrying the statue of the Mother Goddess, they had traveled for two years, crossing unknown territories. Many times they were expelled by hostile tribes, sometimes they were harassed by hungry beasts, punished by storms or droughts. Keeping hope, always walking north, they crossed the great prairies and the desert, until one day the sea stopped their march. Then they discovered that the land they dreamed did not exist, the gods had abandoned it, it no longer rained, and the great flocks had long gone.

It had all been just a dream.

Disoriented and discouraged, the group wandered for some time along the beach line, finding no one who could provide them with any information, and then they went on a journey south.

Three months had passed since the clan had camped in that desolate place. There was nothing special there; simply the existence of a little water in the well had held them back. At first they thought of resting for a few days, to regain strength before continuing the march.

While they were recovering, they sent some explorers in all directions.

Finally, they discovered that there was nothing but desert around them, lack of food, sickness and discouragement brought them down, the emigrants simply waited for the end. Now, after three months, the group had been reduced to fifteen hungry and malnourished individuals, half of them sick. In the morning they buried the old man who had died the day before; apparently even the hyenas had left the region. After the funeral the sorcerer of the group sang sacred songs and lit a bonfire in front of the statue of his goddess, installed on an improvised stone altar next to the wall of the shelter.

The statue represented Mother Earth, a female figure covered with a leopard skin, carrying in her hands the figure of a sacred beetle, symbol of Eternal Life. The origin of the statue was unknown; it was lost in the night of the Times.

Nungal thought of all this as he placed the last stones on the old man's grave. Beside him, Erihen, the chieftain, hit him with a rock.
After distributing the reduced game meat among the group, little was left to feed the hunters that night. They resolved to explore the coast of the sea the next day, hopefully catching some seabirds or fishing. No one in the group had knowledge of sea fishing, originating from the interior of the continent, for them the sea was something unknown. On two occasions they had tried to catch fish with their bone harpoons, but they had always failed.
 They left at dawn, accompanied by the sad gaze of the sick.
On that day the hunters moved farther away than usual, crossing the sea coast towards the east during the whole day. They managed to feed on some seafood they found on the beach, the seagulls took flight before they could get close enough to hunt them with their arrows. Tired and hungry, at nightfall they camped on the beach, a short distance from where the waves became extinct when they met the sand.
The light from the campfire attracted a number of flying insects, which the warriors quickly caught and devoured. A cool sea breeze soothed their bodies, punished by the strong desert sun.
Sitting by the bonfire, Nungal commented, his gaze lost in the flames.
-Do you think that one day we will find the land we are looking for?
Everyone remained silent; Chief Erihen shook his head in pessimism.
-The gods don't want us to reach that place; otherwise we would already be there.
Mumny, the tallest hunter at almost two meters, had lay down on the sand looking at the stars, he said in a calm, almost indifferent voice:
 -That land is over, it no longer exists because the gods do not send rain, without water there is no life.
-We have already arrived at the land of abundance; we have hardly done it too late.
Nungal got up to walk to the first waves of the sea, wet his hands and washed his face with salt water.
-In this sea there are fish, although we don't know how to catch them, our harpoons are useless, and to make nets we would need vegetables and lianas, which don't grow here.
Everyone agreed with his words, Nungal continued - In the same way, there is water, fruits and animals in this land, but we are intruders, we do not know where to hunt, we do not know where to look for fruits.
Mumny laughed sarcastically - Fruits...? Where do the stones come from?
Nergal asked -Should we get out of here?
-Where, perhaps, do you want to return to our land -exclaimed Mumny.
-I don't know, brothers, we must look for the inhabitants, somewhere there must be someone.

-You've lost your head, Nungal, where are the people, if anyone survived in this cursed place!
-Maybe they went to the other side of the sea, we should do the same.
-It's absurd; we can't cross that sea, even if we built several canoes.
-Perhaps the sea has no end; we would never reach the other shore.
-I don't know, brothers, I'm just telling you one thing: if we stay here, we'll all die!
Erihen sat down with his hands embracing his knees, whispered sadly:
- We stopped here just to get our strength back, there are several sick people.
-The first sick have died, then others have fallen ill, we will never recover our strength without food and water- exclaimed Nungal.
Erihen observed his companions, at that moment he was not a chief, just a frightened and confused boy.
- Where will we go? Which way is it?
No one answered; they remained watching the flames of the bonfire, in silence.
Apprehensive, they understood that in that place, they could only find death.

The next day the hunters set out on their way back, following a different path. They left the beach heading straight south, they had not yet explored that region. The landscape was no different, the same desolation, the same endless wind and the reddish dust that covered everything. From time to time someone chewed on the leaves of a bush, to spit them out immediately. The routine of climbing and descending endless hills was interrupted by bushes and rock formations, in which they searched eagerly, trying to capture some lizard or snake.
Mumny cursed aloud when he examined an abandoned nest, hoping to find eggs. Frustrated, he swiped the small building, breaking the branch of the tree.
Halfway through the day they discovered a stream, a miserable thread of water, but it allowed them to quench their thirst and fill their bags with the precious liquid.
A snake, the only thing the hunters could catch near the margin, was the group's only lunch.
-I believe that, if we don't find another place, this stream will always be better than the well where we set up the camp.
-Do you want to bring the whole clan to this place?
- At least water, even if it is scarce, is better, and it doesn't seem to run out.
When they started walking again, they decided to climb a high hill that dominated the landscape at a short distance from the brook. From the top they looked out over the territory, the arid plain extended, seemingly infinite, to the horizon to the east. Looking north, the surface of the sea shone far away, peeking through the bluish hills. Finally, to the west, the plain acquired a yellowish color almost white in the distance; they were sand dunes, until getting lost in the horizon.
No green, no river, no lagoon.

Silently they continued south, planning to follow that direction until sunset, when they would turn west, calculating that in that way they would reach some point near the camp.

The feeling of failure was general; returning to camp empty-handed represented death for several sick comrades.

At a certain moment Nergal cut a cactus that seemed familiar to him, it was similar to those that existed in his native land.

From inside the cactus sprouted a transparent liquid that he drank with caution. Everyone was watching him.

-It's water, a little sweeter, but water at last, the pulp is good!

-Everyone wielded their daggers; the cactus disappeared in a jiffy.

They examined the vicinity, but found no other specimen, and shortly afterwards resumed their march.

In a miserable bush they discovered several lobsters that they disputed, devouring them in a few seconds, some were kept in a leather bag.

Nungal tried to chew the leaf of a small tree that struggled to grow between the stones and the reddish earth, but immediately spat it out, with disgust.

In a few hours it would be dark, they would not reach the camp before dawn, so Erihen considered it convenient to camp there that night, starting the return the next morning. They went towards a stony hollow, there they could find some reptile, the group separated, digging among the stones. Mumny was in charge of lighting a bonfire, there were many branches and dry trunks in the place.

They were searching unsuccessfully, when they saw several hyenas excitedly surrounding something among the rocks. Supposing it could be some wounded animal, the hunters decided to dispute it. As they approached, an arrow from Nungal killed one of them, and their companions threw some stones until the other hyenas left the place grunting threateningly. Mumny threw his usual sarcastic remark:

-I'll finally know the taste of hyena meat.

Erihen approached the rocks cautiously, and then could not contain an exclamation of surprise:

-What the hell is that?

A short distance away, crouching between the rocks, a man of small stature, a little obese, about fifty years old, light-skinned, sporting a broad white beard, was armed with a thick branch, and tried uselessly to hide in a crack between two heavy rocks. He had several wounds on his body, caused by the bites of wild beasts. Passing the initial surprise, the black hunter showed him the palms of the open hands, in sign of peace, the man sighed letting the branch fall. Nungal helped him to get out of the reduced space, to sit him on the ground. The four hunters surrounded him, curious. As usual, Mumny commented:

-Oh, no, I won't eat that, we're not cannibals, brothers.

Erihen silenced him with a gesture; they offered him water, which the old man drank slowly. He pointed to a place about thirty meters below, expressing himself in a dialect that the men understood only in part.
-My bag, my bag.
One of the hunters walked as far as the man indicated, to pick up a leather bag, which he gave to the old man. The man pulled out a handful of olives and dates which he offered to the group. With a faint voice he muttered:
The hyenas despised my provisions, are you hungry? - He carefully examined his rescuers, that gigantic black man was devouring his dates. The old man asked:
-Who are you, where do you come from?
Erihen understood the question and, helped by gestures, explained to the man the odyssey of his group. The man opened his eyes wide when he understood:
-You are lost; you must go to the Great River!
-The Great River? Where there is a great river, here we hardly find stones and sand.
-The Great River, which everyone calls Hiteru or Hapy, will never dry up, it's the river of the gods, the refuge of all men and animals of the world!
The hunters looked at each other; Nungal remembered the conversation of the previous night.
-Where is that river? - asked Mumny, suddenly serious.
-Ten days to the east, always to the east.
The old man's hand was pointing towards the distant sand dunes.
It was getting dark; they led the old man into the hollow where the light of a bonfire shone, and soon after they took care of the old man's wounds as they tried to get more information about the supposed river. Within a short distance Nergal had already skinned the hyena and was about to roast the meat.
At some point Erihen pointed to the bladder with water, asking the old man:
-Where did he get that water?
The old man nodded: -Water in the Great River, yes. There is water in the river.
- No, no. I want to know if there is water nearby.
The old man thought for a moment, and then he seemed to understand the question.
- Water nearby? There is water in the Jackal well- he pointed eastward- A day's march, water in the Jackal well.
The hunters exchanged confused glances.
-Did we get it right or am I wrong?
-He said there is a lake a day's march away.
-And according to him, ten days away is the Great River.
-What are we going to do? - Everyone looked at the leader, Erihen took a deep breath.
-We must go! Here we will barely find death.

Sitting on the floor, the old man watched them, very attentive, Nungal leaned over to his side, smiling:
-I am Nungal, and you?
The old man looked at him, trying to understand, the warrior placed his hand on his chest:
-Nungal- and pointed to the old man's chest, and he finally smiled.
-Ahh, I am Kutum.
-Kutum? - The hunters repeated, and each one gave his name to the smiling old man.
Nungal, sitting with a grave expression next to Kutum, caught his attention by repeating:
-Kutum, is there water there?- he pointed to the east, the old man's eyes shone:
-Yes, water, Jackal's wells, a lot of water.
At dawn Erihen sent Nungal and Nergal in search of the rest of the clan, they should set up camp and lead them all, carrying the statue of the Goddess, to the creek they had found the day before. Leaning on two thick branches, the old man managed to walk, helped by the warriors. The small group undertook the slow march towards the water course. They made the journey calmly, trying to get more information from the old man. Mumny asked him what Erihen must already be thinking:
-What were you doing here, going somewhere?
He must have repeated the question several times, until the old man proved that he understood by opening his eyes wide:
-Oh, of course. I am the healer of the chief Ziuzu, who governs the clan in the swamps of Iteru.
-In the Great River?
-Yes, in the delta of the Great River!
- How did you come to be here, so distant from your land?
-It was a mistake by the great chief Ziuzu. It wasn't my fault, really!
They had interrupted the march to listen to the old man, who continued to speak, sometimes repeating each sentence to make him understood.
-Ziuzu was sick, very sick since he ate the eggs of an unknown animal, offered by the merchants who visit us every year after the floods. To complicate matters, it was our cacique's wedding night; imagine the consequences of that entire problem. He didn't listen to me when I warned him about the risks of eating that crap. The next morning I was with my head full of pustules, which when I touched them were bursting with yellowish pus.
His young wife left her cabin to return to her parents' house, possibly disgusted by the sight of that infected head. It was then that Ziuzu finally decided to listen to my advice.
I knew it was the fault of those cursed eggs. I took care of the chief with ointments of mud, honey and dog saliva. The king gave off a terrible smell, he no

longer had the courage to appear in public. It depressed him to remember that he had lost his wife on the same wedding night.
Everyone looked at each other in surprise. The old man scratched his head before continuing.
-The confusion began when two days later the father of Ziuzu's young wife also appeared in public with his head covered in boils; it seemed to be the same disease.
When he found out, Ziuzu immediately summoned his father-in-law for questioning. The man swore by all the gods that he had not eaten of those eggs, the truth nor did he know they existed. The night his daughter returned home, abandoning Ziuzu, the guy, whose name is Tizqar, got up feeling thirsty. He drank something in the dark before returning to bed. The next morning he was with his head full of pustules and boils. As you will understand, Ziuzu sent two warriors accompanied by the old Tizqar, to confiscate the drink that had supposedly contaminated him. It was a vessel belonging to Tizqar's daughter! It was then that history was complicated by the arrival of a warrior from the upstream fishing clan. He appeared before Ziuzu, asking for forgiveness for the young woman, with whom he was in love. He confessed that everything had been a plan to ruin the young woman's wedding with the chief, a decided wedding between Tizqar and Ziuzu, without consulting the opinion of the maiden, who had been madly in love with the young fisherman for a long time.
At that height nobody walked, everyone surrounded the old man to listen to the outcome of that story. Kutum, seeing that his new friends were very curious, sat on a small stone, pausing briefly, Mumny did not hold back, asking:
-What happened next?
-At first Ziuzu was furious, as you will understand, he ordered the lovers to be locked up in a cabin isolated from the others, kept under strict surveillance. It was there that someone remembered seeing the fisherman a few days before the wedding in the village. On that occasion the man wanted me to make a remedy for scabies he said was punishing his dogs.
Mumny laughed out loud:
-So it was you who made that potion?
Kutum nodded slightly.
-When Ziuzu found out, he wanted to devour me alive, I was trying to cure an illness caused by a potion that was also my work.
-I was placed under surveillance on the outskirts of the village.
-And how did it end up here?
-I come to that, my friend. A moon later, it was announced that the great Ziuzu would do Justice publicly in the esplanade next to the village. People from all the clans came to know Ziuzu's verdict, some thought that the three of us would be personally executed by the humiliated chieftain.

On the morning of the execution Ziuzu appeared, his head covered by a skin, hiding the boils. The couple of lovers and I waited with our hands tied behind our backs, standing in the middle of the esplanade. Ziuzu ordered the young woman and the fisherman to kneel, and then walked slowly towards them, the crowd waited in silence for the outcome of the drama.
Suddenly the great Ziuzu threw a tremendous kick into each lover's ass; the couple fell noisily to the ground. Ziuzu ordered their restraints removed, and granted them freedom right there, exclaiming -Justice has been done!
The crowd, as you will understand, burst out laughing out loud.
Finally the chieftain addressed me, exclaiming:
-You will leave the village and you will not return without having discovered the cure for this filth!
People were throwing fruit at my head when I left the esplanade. I decided to take refuge in the well of the Jackal, to discover an antidote against the cacique's scabies.
- Now I understand. What were you looking for here, a day away from the oasis?
-In this region grows a very rare cactus, which could cure our cacique.
A premonition alarmed Erihen, in an indifferent tone he asked:
-What's that cactus like?
- It's a cactus with few thorns, dark green color, on having cut it a liquid similar to the water sprouts, but of very sweet flavor. Its pulp is delicious, has great medicinal power.
In a casual tone, Mumny denied without looking at it:
-No, I've never seen a cactus like that.
The hunters exchanged a quick glance, without making any comment. Erihen approached Mumny muttering:
-I'm wondering if it would be a good idea to get to that village in the company of this old man.
-Don't worry; half of that story must be a lie.
Shortly before noon they settled into the miserable stream of water flowing from the rocks a few meters above, running until they got lost in the earth, a hundred meters below.
Kutum washed away his wounds by removing the dried blood and soil, which were not really deep, except for a bite that had dilacerating the flesh on the front of the right thigh. The marks on his arms were apparently produced by blows that the old man had suffered against the rocks as he tried to escape from the hyenas.
At the end of the afternoon the rest of the clan arrived, seeing them, Erihen approached Nungal, who was walking a little forward.
-Where is the wizard? The warrior shook his head as he placed the statue of the Goddess on the floor.

-Yesterday the wizard and two women died, we don't know if the cause was hunger or the plague.
When they arrived, the group rushed over the creek, they were thirsty. Elder Kutum opened his leather bag to distribute the last dates and olives to the newcomers.
That night they lit a big bonfire with the intention of attracting nocturnal insects, it was the only food available. Mumny declared with a bitter smile:
-You can't imagine how tasty a hyena is, friends, you missed it.
At dawn they started the march, in total it was a group of five warriors, four women, two children and the old man Kutum, who was walking with difficulty, leaning on a stick. The warriors took turns carrying the statue of the Goddess. The group moved slowly eastward, walking across the arid plain, under a strong sun in a cloudless sky.
They had enough water for the march, which the old man said would last only a day.
At dusk, Kutum reported that the well was not more than two hours away, resolved to continue the march during the night, illuminated by a waning moon. They arrived without any inconvenience at Jackal well, it was an oval-shaped lake, about twenty meters long, with crystalline water, surrounded by a pile of palm trees, different types of trees, some minor shrubs and many papyrus. The old man suggested to them to light a bonfire, warning about the possible presence of carnivores, he led them to the small coat that he had raised some time ago.
 Erihen found that the old man had indeed been there before, that corroborated his whole story. To general surprise, Kutum came out of the small hut with several pieces of salted and smoked meat, which he distributed to his new friends.
-I have several traps installed around here that sometimes allow me to have meat.
With thirst quenched and fed, for the first time in a long time the survivors of Harahan's clan slept in peace, without feeling tormented by hunger and uncertainty.

With the first lights of dawn the group awoke, pleasantly surprised by the joyful bustle of hundreds of birds singing among the trees of the oasis, the place was full of life, the travelers marveled at the spectacle. Elder Kutum dedicated himself to cleaning his wounds, using a kind of green ointment, which gave off a strong aroma of vegetables. Observing that the black hunters carried their small bows on their backs, the old man pointed to the desert.
-If you want to hunt an animal, now is the right time, I have enough salt to prepare it.

Mumny and Nungal were immediately interested in what the old man said:
-Nothing would please us more than to hunt our food.
-Then they must take advantage of the dawn, when some animals approach to quench their thirst in the lower well.
-Is there another well?
-Of course, a little lower down is where all the animals drink," he pointed to his left. The two warriors, with their bows in their hands, were already on their way to the place. The old man hastened to warn.
-There is also a forest around the lake, in which carnivores often lurk, be careful.
In a few minutes the warriors completed the hundred meters separating the two small lakes, both had separated to cover a larger area, keeping about twenty meters between them. When they were less than fifteen meters from the first trees, a gazelle began to flee, noticing Mumny's approach.
The animal was trying to escape by running fast away from Mumny, would pass within a short distance of his companion, who already had the bow ready. For an experienced hunter like Nungal, that gazelle did not represent a difficult target, he shot an arrow with deadly precision, correcting the flank of the animal. The gazelle still ran for about thirty meters before dropping dead. At that moment several gazelles emerged from the other side, fleeing swiftly to the meadow without giving the hunters time to react. An antelope suddenly appeared among the vegetation to trot into the desert, passing between them. Mumny was in an excellent position; he threw his arrow before Nungal turned his body to that side. The small arrow reached the animal in the middle of the jump. The antelope advanced a few meters until it finally succumbed.
As they approached the gazelle's body, a group of antelope rushed into the desert, the hunters gazed at them without moving, the two captured prey would be enough to feed the whole group and there would still be plenty of meat for the journey. They didn't hunt uselessly; they didn't feel pleasure in killing.
 An hour later the hunters returned to the spring, the body of the gazelle hanging from a thick branch transported between them, to the joy of the group. When Nungal reported that they also hunted an antelope, the women and children seemed to go mad, happy. Nergal and a boy went immediately in search of the antelope; they had to prevent some predator from seizing the prey.
Kutum examined the small arrow he pulled from the gazelle.
-It is astonishing that a single insignificant little arrow should produce such forceful results.
-What kills is not the arrow, but the poison- revealed Nungal, as he drew the wand with his dagger.
-Poison? - Kutum quickly removed the finger he had placed on the tip of the arrow, the old man's expression provoked a smile in the hunter.

-Don't worry; it's a poison that loses effect quickly, evacuated with the animal's blood, leaving no traces. With the knife he made two cuts in the tendons of the gazelle, to introduce a resistant strip of leather.
-I would even say that the poison leaves a delicious taste in the meat- added Mumny behind the old man's back, who analyzed the arrow in his hands, squinting.
The gazelle had been hung from the hind legs to be skinned. A short distance away, the warriors proceeded to hang the body of the antelope, larger and heavier than the first prey. It was a festive day for the group, everyone could finally get fed up with food and even prepare salted meat for the long day they would soon have to face. It seemed that the days of deprivation and famine were over.

Four days later the group began their journey through the desert.
All felt optimistic, had enough provisions, and the days they stayed in the oasis served to recover strength, Kutum was already walking normally, his wounds showed a pink coloration, without pus.
For ten days they walked eastward, keeping the sea a few hours to their left. The journey went on without much news; a herd of jackals accompanied them in the distance, without daring to attack, just waiting for someone to separate from the group, which did not happen.
When there were two days to reach the Great River, the landscape was different; a green carpet of grass covered much of the meadow, populated by herds of herbivores and flocks of birds that crossed the sky. The vegetation was abundant, announcing the proximity of the River.
Two days later, climbing a green hill covered by palm trees, the group was able to contemplate for the first time Iteru, the Great River, God protector of Life.
Bordered by a belt of dense green vegetation, it ran smoothly and majestically to the north. They walked through the forest for half an hour, to finally approach the margin; numerous crocodiles entered the water noisily, disappearing beneath the surface. In some nearby trees, the pink plumage of dozens of flamingos and other waterfowl stood out. A wide strip of black earth, partially covered with grass, bordered the riverbed. From the reed a small bird with its deep red plumage and a long black beak watched them. Swarms of insects flew through the place, while the song of numerous birds invisible among the vegetation was heard. In the center of the river, two huge hippos looked like big rocks emerging over the water, when part of their heads appeared, one of them opened an enormous mouth and both disappeared under the surface.
Erihen approached the shore, several sinister eyes watching him from the reeds. About twenty meters away, a huge crocodile rested on the ground a short distance from the margin. Erihen observed that the animal remained completely

motionless, allowing several birds to traverse its body, tasting small parasites among its scales. At one point the chieftain could see that the crocodile had opened its huge mouth and remained calm as two birds entered its fearsome jaws to devour the remains of food extracted between the crocodile's teeth. Erihen had already witnessed this phenomenon in his homeland, but he was always surprised to see the collaboration between such different species.

-Be careful as you approach the water, I see many crocodiles- he warned the children, lifting a finger with a severe expression.

The old man Kutum approached the tree under whose shade the chieftain stood. He gestured to the north.

-In that direction, less than two days away, is the village of Ziuzu, the Snail Eaters, in the river delta. Pointing to the other side, he added -And there, to the south, live several groups of fishermen, they are small peaceful clans, with which Ziuzu maintains trade.

Those days of coexistence had contributed to improve communication, in fact the dialect spoken by Kutum had numerous words common to the language of Erihen and his people, and each dialogue increased mutual understanding.

Nungal sat on a fallen log a short distance away.

-I think that up there would be a good place to set up the camp- he pointed to a small forest in a high place, a short distance from the river. Kutum looked at the ground of the place, noting that the earth was reddish.

-The whole expanse of black earth is covered by the river during the annual flood, so I'm seeing the water not rise to the top of that hill.

-Then it's a good place to camp permanently- said Erihen-That's where we'll build our village.

For the rest of the day they built the first huts, cut long branches, collected wide leaves from aquatic plants, and gathered a good supply of firewood. Finally, they built a small stone altar on which they installed the statue of the Goddess Earth, which would be visible from a great distance from the other side of the river.

-It will make a strong impression on whoever sails in front of our village.

-Our village- repeated Erihen, with a smile, next to him, Nungal was also happy, remembering the difficult previous months in the desert.

After a quick incursion into the edge of the forest, the hunters shot down several preys that guaranteed food for the next few days. Mumny was happy.

-The forest provides the perfect place to surprise the herds that graze in the meadow, this is a paradise.

The next morning, Kutum drove Erihen and Nungal to the delta, soon to meet the most powerful chieftain in the region.

The trio walked north along the river, the vegetation on the banks thickening as they approached the delta lowlands. Hippos and a variety of waterfowl abounded. Certain undulations on the surface of the river revealed the presence of huge fish, Kutum commented, excited to have returned.

-After tasting the fish and snails of the village, you will never want to eat anything else.

ZIUZU AND THE SNAIL EATERS

That afternoon the three travelers found two fishermen who were removing fish from a trap, next to them, a light canoe of reeds and papyrus was on the shore, inside the fishermen had deposited a good number of fish.

Kutum approached by raising his open hand as a form of greeting, the two guys responded in the same way. They were light-skinned individuals with long black hair and beards, wearing only a leather thong.

As they approached, Erihen offered them dry meat and water, the fishermen immediately demonstrated their hospitality by placing several snails on a small board, which Kutum savored with pleasure, praising their taste with exaggerated gestures, Erihen and Nungal watched the snails with suspicion. Nungal put one's contents in one's mouth, savoring cautiously, under Harahan's attentive gaze. Noticing the gesture of approval of his companion, the chief decided to taste the food. In front of the inquisitive look of the fishermen, Erihen imitated the gestures of Kutum, approving the flavor of the snail, which drew a smile from his hosts. Their dialect was the same as Kutum's, so they communicated without difficulty. The fishermen were receptive to the group, although their expressions turned gloomy as they warned them about the red-haired white men who feed on people.

-They live in the mountains beyond the horizon, they always attack by surprise, they show no mercy to children or the elderly, and they take the women with them.

The second fisherman nodded, supporting the statements of his companion.

-Sometimes they arrive at night, to steal our meat and our women, destroying what they cannot take with them. When they were informed that the travelers were going to their village, the fishermen indicated the place where they could cross the river to reach the arm of water where the community rose.

Shortly after, the trio continued their journey, walking until dusk.

That night they spent the night at the edge of the Great River, in a place where they found no signs of crocodiles. They lit a bonfire and rested the whole night. At dawn they continued their march for a couple of hours until they reached the place indicated by the fishermen. It was a small pier, some villagers looked at them with curiosity, they looked like all the inhabitants of the region, wearing only a leather thong. Upon learning the fate of the travelers, a boy offered to transport them to the other side of the river arm. The crossing did not take more than ten minutes. Once on the opposite bank, they walked for an hour, finally

Kutum pointed to a lagoon a short distance from the river. On its banks, they could contemplate numerous people dedicated to the most varied activities.
-We are here, my friends- the elderly man announced without hiding his joy.
Shortly afterwards they arrived at a wide esplanade, adjacent to the village of the snail eaters, which had been built in the centre of a lagoon of swampy banks, built on wooden stakes - stilt houses - was surrounded by a wall of sharp bamboo.
In the esplanade circulated a good number of people dedicated to their daily chores, making nets and ropes, salting fish and meat, felling and transporting huge logs and firewood. The outsiders did not seem to attract attention; those people were used to receiving visitors, usually interested in exchanging products.
Kutum extended a hand pointing towards the village.
The natives claim that the Red-Haired Men are not good swimmers; they only once tried to attack the village. They suffered a punishment so great that they never returned.
Agile canoes sailed the waters, each manned by two or three fishermen.
The natives are invincible on board their canoes, the Red-Haired Men fear them.
Erihen observed that the last stretches of the bridge could be removed, isolating the village from unwanted visitors. Kutum approached a pair of warriors who, armed with a spear and a small triangular shield of leather, guarded the entrance to the bridge.
Recognizing it, one of the guards smiled, sarcastic.
-Kutum has returned, Ziuzu will be happy to see him! The other warrior also smiled amusingly, examining the two tall black-skinned individuals, armed only with small bows on their backs.
-Who are your companions, old man?
-They are from a people in the south who wish to pay tribute to the mighty Ziuzu.
The sentry gestured, lifting his spear in the direction of a pair of guards at the other end of the bridge.
-They will lead them in the village - as the old man was about to walk following the black warriors, the guard tapped him on the shoulder.
-Good luck, Kutum.
The village seemed enormous to the visitors, they calculated that it should have more than a hundred inhabitants, it looked clean and well organized, Kutum seemed nervous, because he wouldn't stop talking - They say that in the flood season, the lake waters communicate with the Great River, which they call Hiteru. When the waters go down, hundreds of huge fish get caught in the lake, which happens every year.
They had reached the other side of the bridge where two warriors armed with spears and the characteristic triangular leather shields awaited them. They walked a short distance to a cabin that in no way differed from the others; at the door Ziuzu was waiting for them, sitting on a bench built with a huge trunk.

He was an individual in his forties, medium in stature, quite potbellied, with a nice face and an easy and generous smile underneath a huge round nose.

He wore a long antelope-skin tunic. A necklace of colorful pebbles adorned her neck. Visitors immediately looked at the chief's head, there were no boils, hardly any scars, but there was no hair either.

Realizing that the visitors were examining his head, Ziuzu smiled, looking cruelly at the old man:

-Ahhh, Kutum...Kutum. You old pretender, you have dared to return.

-Hello, mighty Ziuzu, I see you have finally improved, I always knew.

The chief seemed to have forgotten the presence of the black warriors.

-I've lost all my hair because of you, son of a cow!

-But you no longer suffer with those pustules, Ziuzu... My medicine finally cured you.

The chieftain ran a hand over his head, caressing the scars left by the boils.

-It's true, that cured me. But I've lost my beautiful hair!

-Look on the bright side of that: you don't have to worry about lice.

Ziuzu lifted his shoulders, reflecting for a moment:

-I don't suffer with lice either, it's true. This is an evil that tortures our people, especially in this region of swamps.

Kutum bowed his head, humbly - To see that you are well makes me very happy, my king.

-Who are your companions, you crazy old man?

-The great chief Erihen and his best warrior, Nungal. They come from a distant land to the south, which he had to abandon after suffering severe punishment from their gods. They wish to settle under the protection of the Great River.

Ziuzu looked carefully at his visitors, apparently he liked them because he nodded his approval, smiling.

-The Great River always welcomes those who come in peace.

-We come in peace; we just want a place to live- answered Erihen, speaking for the first time.

-Is it a large group?

-A dozen, sir, we lost most of our brothers during the trip.

Ziuzu raised his right arm:

- You are welcome. I am interested in populating the banks of the Great River with friendly clans who will help us reject invasions - He paused, opening both arms, with a broad smile - The only tribute I wish to receive will be your surplus products, you will receive in return our fish, wood, fruits and the help you need, in the same proportion. That's how we relate to all riversides; the trade has been good for everyone. However... -new pause, the king leaned the body forward- it's important that you collaborate in the defense of the territory, we need warriors.

He extended his arms again, adding - Our rich land is coveted by barbarian peoples, we have already suffered attacks in the past, we always manage to reject them, but the enemy strengthens, increases in number, becomes more and more daring. We must be united to protect the Great River that is my only condition.
-We thank you for your hospitality, Ziuzu; we will know how to defend the Goddess Earth.
The caciques sealed their friendship simply with a hug. Ziuzu forgave Kutum, who was authorized to return from exile, although he forbade him to settle in the village.

As Ziuzu offered them transport for the following morning, they camped in the vicinity of the village, at the end of the esplanade that separated the lake from the river, under the shade of the trees, where the dense vegetation of the swamp began. The fishermen who were to transport them arrived shortly after, handing them two huge fish promised to return the next morning to begin the journey. The black warriors watched the intense activity in the delta lands, small groups found themselves felling trees, others built boats, some women carried reed baskets with vegetables, fruits or eggs, children transported firewood or simply had fun around the women, accompanied by dogs.
In the numerous arms of the Delta agile canoes of rushes and papyrus seemed to fly over the greenish waters that slid lazily towards the sea. Some fishermen leaned over to examine traps set in pools near the banks. Huge hundred-year-old trees hung down their long branches caressing the surface of the water. From time to time a bird would submerge like a multicolored ray to emerge soon after, carrying a fish that would calmly devour on a branch.
After spending so much time in the desert, that place revealed itself as a true paradise for visitors.
 Erihen was about to clean a fish with his dagger.
-What did you think?
Nungal was sitting on a fallen log in the small improvised camp, lighting a bonfire.
-He's a good leader; I think he'll make an excellent neighbor.
- Ziuzu does not seem to be ambitious, even though he governs a large, well-organized village.
With quick movements, plucking a rain of sparks by rubbing two stones, Nungal lit a bonfire, a timid column of smoke rose from the small heap of dry grass.
Erihen muttered:
-But their snails are rubbish.
-We agree on that.
Both smiled, the flames were already rising in the bonfire, Nungal added small twigs that began to crackle.

Kutum had lay down on the grass with both hands behind his head, his face was exaggeratedly serious.
-Maybe I should raise a hut here, outside the village, I could fish and...
Erihen, seeing the old man Kutum depressed by the ban on staying in the village of the Snail Eaters, placed his hand on the old man's shoulder.
-Kutum, you are already a member of our group, we want you to stay with us, your knowledge will be of great help.
-I will personally take care of building your hut, my friend- promised Nungal.
The words of the chief Erihen immediately transformed the mood of the old man, who was suddenly happy, opening a wide smile.
So sudden was his change of mood that Nungal and Erihen exchanged a funny look, the joy seemed to awaken the old man's tongue, which led to an endless monologue.
-From the swamp that surrounds the lake, the natives get crabs and an infinite number of small animals, the lake is their world. They use bows a little larger than yours, which shoot arrows of a medium size, with deadly aim, hunting birds, fish and rodents. Braiding a plant that abounds on the margins, they make nets and traps for fishing. Have I already told you about the enormous Perch? It's the biggest fish in the river.
The two friends were already moving away from the chit chattering, to start cleaning the fish, avoiding listening to the endless stories of Kutum.
-Hey! Have I told you about the bread that these people cook, using the sun's rays? Haven't I mentioned it yet? All right, they do it that way...

MOSTAGGEDA, THE CROSSBRED.

It could not be called a village, it was just a settlement formed by huts of branches and mud, built in a semicircle around a grotto with several entrances and without much depth, on the wall of a large rocky hill. Each cave was used to enlarge the space occupied by the whole, some bonfires burned inside each cavity. Numerous palms and shrubs grew around the huts. About fifty meters away began the great lake, which in the distant future would be known as the Dead Sea. Its dimensions were larger at that time, forming part of a set of lakes that extended to the south, to the vicinity of the Gulf of Aqaba. At its northern end, the great lake communicated with the Sea of Galilee, where the reduction of the lake began to give rise to the future Jordan River. This vast territory was the largest source of salt in the entire region and was firmly controlled by the Red-Haired Men.
The village was a group of several communities, direct descendants of the first migratory waves of Humanity, which inhabited since remote times the region around the great lake. Long ago, pushed by one of the numerous climatic changes,

their ancestors had arrived to the region, escaping from the advance of the snows.

At that time the territory was a true paradise, the abundant rain had formed a complete ecosystem, with abundant vegetation and varied animal life. The easy life propitiated the peaceful coexistence between the different clans.

But nothing is forever, one day the rains began to reduce, until they ended completely. Rivers and lagoons dried up, vegetation was reduced and the animals emigrated.

Competition had begun for the increasingly scarce resources.

About thirty Red-Haired Men inhabited that village, along with about fifteen slave women, captured among the clans of neighboring territories, with physical characteristics clearly different from their captors. For the most part, they had long, deep black hair and fair skin, tanned by life outdoors. Others, to a lesser extent, had black skin and curly hair, combed differently, forming a huge ball over the head, which increased their apparent stature. Many slaves were accompanied by children of different ages, while they dedicated themselves to the most varied activities. Some of these children had features similar to the Red Hair Warriors; others had the racial characteristics of their mothers. In strategic places, robust warriors with light hair, chestnut or reddish, stood guard supported by their heavy spears.

No dogs were seen. There was also no laughter or conversation among the women, only a few young children played around their mothers, and their cheerful bustle contrasted with the austere atmosphere of the place.

In a space close to the huts, the remains of animals consumed by the inhabitants were accumulated, among those remains diverse human bones could be distinguished, revealing the sinister practice of cannibalism among the Red-Haired Men.

Leaning over a magnificent lioness skin, Mostaggeda used the weight of his body to rub the scraper harder, sweat washed over his face.

He was a teenager, between fifteen and sixteen years old, taller than the youngsters of his age, reaching one meter and sixty, the size considered normal for an adult Red Hair. His hair was reddish and his eyes were bright blue, but his slightly darker skin revealed his half blood condition. He wore a simple thong of wild goatskin that covered his waist up to his knees, leaving his torso naked, where some scars were already visible.

From the nearest hut his mother's voice was heard.

-Son, you must come out of the sun, place that skin in the shade of the hut.

-You know he's forbidden me; he won't let me out of here.

The woman, whose name was Mashda, came out of the hut. She appeared to be in her forties, deep wrinkles furrowed her face, the unmistakable mark of a life of suffering. She was very thin, a little over a meter and a half tall, her long hair, once very black, was now shaded in grey.

Like her son, she wore a goatskin skirt, which exposed her torso. The white skin was intensely tanned. Mashda walked to where the young man worked to reach a large sea snail, in which she carried water. The boy must have been thirsty, because he drank to the last drop, before continuing to work.
-I will ask him not to torture you under the sun!
Mostaggeda lifted his head to answer, but was interrupted when he saw a strong individual emerge from the other side of the hut, with intense red hair, covered with a zebra skin. Several feathers adorned his hair; he exhibited a braided leather necklace, from which hung the skull of an eagle, dyed ochre.
With arrogant movements, he carried several skins that he deposited at the entrance of the hut, interrupting the dialogue between mother and son to interrogate the woman with a simple gesture of his head. The woman, nervous, replied.
- Melemana, allows Mostaggeda to finish the skin in the shade.
Melemana did not answer; he bent down to examine the skin of the lion, next to the teenager. The man remained thoughtful for a moment, shook his head with a disapproving gesture and without uttering a word he struck a strong slap in the face of the young man, who was violently thrown to the side. The woman put both hands in her mouth, not daring to scream.
-Everyone knows that a skin must be tanned under the sun- he muttered softly.
Melemana straightened up, lifting the lion's skin to examine it, and closed her fist tightly, threatening.
-You're not doing a good job, you're ruining that skin!
With firm steps he left without looking at the woman. She ran to protect her son, who refused her help with a brusque gesture, wiping a thread of blood from his mouth with the back of his hand.
Without saying a word, Mostaggeda leaned over to continue scraping the skin, under the strong sun.

Menuttaui cut very small pieces of meat, which he slowly put into the old man's mouth, which he chewed for a few seconds before swallowing. The man would be about fifty years old, a very advanced age for the average life of the time. His hair was chestnut, his body was still sturdy, of short stature; his tiny gray eyes watched the girl as she cut the meat on a flat board, placed on top of his knees. The girl sat on a stone beside the bed of skins and dry leaves where the old man rested. They were inside a simple, circular hut. The only adornment was an antelope skull with long horns, hanging over the head of the bed, covered with fluffy skins.
The man opened his mouth to receive a new portion of meat.
The girl wore the same skirt common to all the slaves in the village, made of wild goatskin, a relatively easy animal to catch, very abundant in the region. The man

made a gesture which the girl immediately understood, and bent down to lift the bladder, checking that it was empty.
-Oh, I'm sorry; I forgot to bring water before lunch.
The old man smiled, and raised one hand to gently caress the young woman's black hair - Don't worry, just go get it.
Menuttaui rose quickly, bladder in hand, smiled briefly at the old man with a loving look.
- I won't be long- she walked briskly under the sun to the well, which was no more than thirty yards from the hut. He leaned over the well to submerge the bladder, watching the bubbling of the water, as the reflection on the surface revealed a familiar face to his back. As she turned, the girl greeted her friend.
-Hello Mostaggeda.
The young man leaned over to his side to remove water with a turtle shell.
-The damned man hit me again.
Mostaggeda washed his face with his hand, before pouring the contents of the shell over his head. The liquid relieved the heat for a moment.
She placed a hand on the young man's arm - what happened?
- My father is a damned animal; I don't know how long I can bear it!
-You must avoid provoking him; you know that his reactions are brutal.
-He's a monster who enslaved my mother and hates me!
- I must go, I'm feeding Turahena, and we'll talk later.
-Tonight, Menuttaui, in the usual place.
-We'll meet you there.
The girl walked fast to the hut, the sand burning her bare feet at every step. Mostaggeda drank a good sip of water and filled the shell again to transport the fresh liquid to his hut. Inside, his mother cut several onions, while in a small bonfire on the outside; lentils were cooked in a rustic earthenware container. The woman offered an onion that the boy chewed without saying a word.
-You are as taciturn as your father; will you tell me if you liked it?
The young man seemed to return from his thoughts.
-You know I like cooked onions, where did you get them?
-Your father collected them yesterday, found several plants on the other side of the rocky ground down there- she pointed to the north. The woman was interrupted when she saw that her son was no longer eating.
The young man placed the rest of the onion on the table. She sat on the edge of the bed with a sad expression.
-Don't reject the food Melemana places on our table, he will be challenged.
-He is not your husband, he's your master, and he has enslaved us. With the years you got used to this damned situation!
-Don't say that, if he listens to you he can kill you, my son.
The young man left the hut to sit outside in the shade. The lentils boiled in the clay pot, Mashda removed the pot from the fire, looking at the boy:

-I found the lentils near the lake, in the land of the fig trees. Will you deign to eat them?
-When I'm hungry. I promise you, Mother.
The woman smiled, caressing the boy's head.
At that moment there was a joy coming from the other side of the village, several children running to the place where Susuda, the warrior, arrived proudly displaying the product of a hunt, an enormous wild boar that two warriors were carrying hanging from a stick. Arriving at the center of the village, the warrior shouted with a loud voice: - Agga! - A young slave reached a large snail with water, the warrior drank spilling some of the water, which ran through his jaw to spill down his chest. At that moment Agga came out of her hut, smiling.
-What have you hunted this time, great Susuda?
Susuda gestured proudly to the boar.
-I'll save the heart and kidneys for you, Agga! For the future leader of the tribe, the best warrior!
Agga placed her right hand on her friend's shoulder as a sign of gratitude.
At her side, the woman offered him water once more, Susuda rejected her with a derogatory gesture, hitting the slave's arm, and the snail fell to the ground.
Silently the woman disappeared quickly between the huts, frightened.
Susuda walked several steps with a defiant attitude, directing fierce glances towards the hut of the old chief Turahena, repeating very loudly, almost shouting:
-Agga is our true chief; he's the warrior who always leads us to victory!
At that moment Melemana approached, observed the hunters, made an exaggerated gesture of approval contemplating the wild boar and went to Susuda, with the intention of praising his hunt. Susuda barely gave him an indifferent brief glance before turning his back on him to enter his hut, followed by his hunters. Visibly humiliated, Melemana quickly returned to his hut.
Sitting in the shade, Mostaggeda had not lost any detail of what had happened.
-The Red-Haired men don't just hate their slaves; they also hate each other- thought the young man as he fiddled with several pebbles in a distracted gesture.
Inside his cabin, the old Turahena had listened to the dialogue between his warriors without showing emotion. Sensing Menuttaui's anguished expression; he smiled with a brief gesture, downplaying the importance of what had happened.
Turahena had always been a brave chieftain, leading his people's raids into neighboring villages, just as his father had long ago.
He was always respected and obeyed by all, his enemies feared him.
That situation remained that way, until that fateful day, during a hunt. A wild horse wounded him badly when it hit him with a sharp kick in the waist. Since then his health broke, he felt difficulty to walk, he found it difficult to participate

in the raids. In spite of everything, Turahena kept leading the clan, supported by most of his warriors, who respected his decisions.

When he found it impossible to accompany the hunters, his best warrior, Agga, began to replace him. Little by little, Agga conquered a group of warriors who supported him, and were favored during the distribution of slaves and received the best part of booty. With the passing of time, there were many who believed that Turahena should cede power to its main warrior. The rivalry between the two was accentuated after the recent attack in which Agga returned with eight captives and an abundant looting.

Turahena had lost her old slave, who died a short time ago. For a few days he remained under the care of his faithful warriors, but could not continue in such conditions, the cacique needed a young slave. For that reason, when Agga returned, proudly displaying the spoils of her victory, Turahena approached slowly, supported by a warrior, to examine the women. Arriving in front of Menuttaui, he observed her for a few moments, with a gesture of approval.

-This will be my new slave.

Agga intervened making a negative gesture - She is the youngest of the group, she belongs to me by right!

It was a clear challenge to the authority of the chief, everyone watched the old man, awaiting his reaction.

It was not necessary for Turahena to respond, Puanuna, a young warrior, stood beside the chief with his spear. Immediately, brothers Darana and Dabagha also demonstrated their support for Turahena. In a few minutes, more than ten warriors challenged Agga's group, surrounding his chief with firmness. Appearing somewhat indolent some leaned on their spears, smiling sarcastically. There was a tense silence for a few moments.

Susuda consulted her leader with a glance, waiting for a gesture to rush against the cacique. Agga, however, let her guard down and smiled briefly, raising her open right hand; he took a step back:

-The best slave is for our cacique- Agga pushed Menuttaui gently towards Turahena.

The tension seemed to dissipate.

In return for Agga's "courtesy", the chief allowed the remainder of the spoils to be distributed as Agga arranged. From that day on Menuttaui was the property of the cacique. Contrary to the expectations of the girl, who was prepared to endure the punishments and abuses normally suffered by slaves, Turahena treated her like a daughter, possibly as a result of the illness that afflicted her. The cacique's health weakened day by day. The girl suffered a hard blow to know that her mother died that same day, the woman could not bear the terrible journey and the idea of becoming a slave. When she was led to the hut of the warrior to whom she was awarded by Agga, the woman collapsed, before the indifferent gaze of her captors. From that moment on, Menuttaui understood that Turahena represented his only chance of survival and decided to silently endure the new living conditions. She would be an obedient and docile slave, studying the warriors of Red Hair, should learn their customs, speak their language and know inch by inch that territory. Only then would he be able to find the best way to escape. Deep within his heart, Menuttaui cherished hope, knew that Hor was alive and would not rest until he found it.

During the nights, in the solitude of her miserable bed, formed by a single goatskin, lying on the floor of the hut, the young woman cried in silence.

She remembered the happy days, which those brutes had ended in blood and fire. As she looked up she could see Turahena, who slept on her fluffy bed a short distance from the girl, agitated by fever. Menuttaui felt a strong desire to stab that individual, chief of those cursed, but that would be foolishness, she said to herself. She needed that man to stay alive, to gain time.

However, in spite of the careful care of the girl, the chieftain did not seem to improve, in the last days no longer left the bed, Menuttaui had to feed him personally.

But Turahena remained lucid; he kept the power through his most faithful warriors, who were responsible for enforcing the orders of the chief.

It was a moonless night; a complete darkness diluted the faint silhouettes of cabins, palm trees and the accidents of the terrain. Mostaggeda knew that the warriors stood guard at the two entrances to the village. Inside, the slaves and their children could circulate without problems; they allowed everyone without exception, and without asking questions. Nevertheless, the group had chosen for their evening meetings a place outside the village, where they would hardly be allowed to frequent accompanied by a guard during the day. At night they would never allow it, the slaves risked severe punishment, even death, so Mostaggeda thanked the gods for that darkness. The young man slipped between the huts easily dodging the guards, not the first time he did so.

He could not contain a smile as he jumped like a feline behind a undulating terrain, where he stood to walk normally, in that place he could no longer be seen from the entrance to the village.

When he arrived at the meeting place, Menuttaui and two other young men were waiting for him. They used to gather, sheltered at night, under that group of palm trees and bushes, which hid them from the view of others. Those brief moments of illusory freedom represented a lot for those young slaves. At times they managed to steal a little food that they divided among themselves. Tonight Menuttaui had laid out on a stone a sea shell containing dates, cooked lentils and a little dried meat. Mostaggeda leaned over to place a cooked onion, which was immediately cut into small pieces to mix with the lentils. Hemman, a boy about twelve years old, offered several small fish, muttering with pleasure:

-Wow, today we have a banquet.
- All right, then attack!- Whispered the third boy in the group jovially, named Agrinnes, a boy just ten years old. Of all of them, as soon as Menuttaui had known life outside that village, the others were the sons of slaves, they had been born there and their lives were limited to the surroundings of the lake. The girl used to remember aloud her previous life, recounting the customs and daily life of her people in the distant mountains of the south, astonishing her friends, who listened to her in silence.
Her voice became melancholy when she mentioned her loved ones; inside she kept alive the hope of escaping captivity. Perhaps Hor would arise suddenly to rescue her.
-Hor...What would have happened to the boy? Did he also find death at the hands of those bastards?
Menuttaui remembered perfectly the way he had traveled to reach the village, he felt able to return by his own means, he should hardly wait for an opportunity. His home was somewhere distant to the south.
- You have been very fortunate to be selected by the old chief Turahena, he must be the only one of those brutes who possesses a heart - The comment interrupted his thoughts; in captivity, Mostaggeda had become a good friend.
-This afternoon Susuda challenged old Turahena again- commented the apprehensive girl.
-That has become frequent, Agga longs for power! I have seen him humiliate my father in front of everyone; he will be a terrible tyrant if he gets the leadership. You must take care of the old chieftain's health, that's important not just for you, but for all of us.
- You're right, Mostaggeda, I'll never stop thanking Turahena.
 The young woman reminded her mother not to resist captivity. She promised herself that her destiny would be different.
The group quickly devoured everything they had laid on the stone, all of them hardly Menuttaui did not suffer from hunger, the sons of slaves were treated like bastards, with the exception of those who preserved the racial characteristics that Red-Haired Men demanded of their descendants. The young woman tried to divert the conversation to less worrisome matters:
-All right, boys, did we continue the discussion from the night before?
All laughed softly, trying not to provoke noises that could attract the attention of the guards, the girl continued, with an exaggeratedly solemn gesture.
-Why can't these monsters have daughters?
Among chuckles, the boys mentioned possibilities ranging from a curse of the gods, to suggesting strange sexual positions that caused an explosion of contained laughter.
- Damn, only males are born around here - Murmured Menuttaui imitating the movements of Red Hair men.

-I am the great Susuda, the best hunter of mice and lobsters! Hemman walked swinging his arms, imitating a monkey. Little Agrinnes had tears in his eyes, trying to contain his laughter.
-Shhhhh, calm down, they can hear us, and that would put us in serious trouble!
 They remained having fun for an hour, that brief sensation of freedom became something important for the group, which recovered energies to support their destiny every morning. Around midnight they sneaked back to their huts.

No one could tell who had discovered the properties of that drink. Possibly a collector deposited in some place without protection, a basket with seeds, during the incursions by the fields where the wild grain grew, in the season of the harvest. Wielding their obsidian sickles with wooden handles, the slaves, their children and some guardians selected the ears of wheat, flax, millet or barley, which were still relatively abundant in the region, despite the scarce rains.
Sometimes they were forced to walk up to seven days to reach the land where the cereals grew, often disputed with other clans, getting to fight real battles. In order not to waste time, the collected grain was deposited in some hidden place, and the group went to other collection places. At the end of the harvest, they returned, collecting the grain hidden along the way.
Probably the fortunate accident that changed human life occurred when a sudden rain flooded a container, or part of the grain was accidentally spilled into a well. However it happened, the result was the fermentation of the barley seeds.
When someone returned in search of the hidden grain, he found the seeds fermented by moisture; in those conditions they were not usable.
Instead of getting rid of them, he - or she- we will never know that - was probably hungry or thirsty and drank some of the liquid... it was the first time that a human being drank beer, possibly suffering the first drunkenness of History.
That discovery spread among the clans of the region.
Since then, the Red-Haired Men waited anxiously for the harvesting season of this cereal, reserving part of the harvest to ferment it. During the Full Moon they celebrated a banquet in which everyone got drunk after practicing cannibalism, consuming the meat of prisoners.
For this reason, Agga and Susuda were enthusiastic about the arrival of the group of slaves carrying bags and baskets overflowing with barley, wheat and flax.
The guards led two prisoners, young individuals, with brown skin and black hair, members of the tribes of the far north, with whom they used to dispute hunting and collecting territories. Susuda examined the prisoners with a gesture of approval. Both were led to one of the stone caves, where they were tied to a stake. Agga ordered to give them plenty of water and food.
From his hut, Menuttaui contemplated discreetly, while he ground the wheat with a stone mortar, making flour that, mixed with water and arranged on small

depressions excavated on the rocks, would be cooked by the strong solar rays obtaining in this way the bread. It was Turahena favorite food.

The young woman knew that the arrival of the cereal collectors meant the manufacture of that damned drink that transformed those men, and everything would culminate in a macabre ritual of cannibalism. The captives had only four days to live, the time it would take for the grain to ferment. It would coincide with the first night of the Full Moon.

The young woman did not imagine that it was also four days before her relative security ended.

That morning four hunters were looking for traces of animals some distance from the village. That hunt had really been Agga's pretext for leaving the village without attracting the attention of Turahena and his men.

While her two companions examined the slope of the hill, rummaging with their spears in a fox hole beneath the stones, Agga and Susuna had sat in the shade of a little palm forest. They were discussing the final details of a plan that should eventually eliminate Chief Turahena, placing Agga in power.

With brief gestures, glancing around to make sure of their privacy, the two men talked for several minutes. They finally seemed to have agreed, because they stood up with a satisfied expression, walking to meet their two companions, who discovered that the fox's burrow had a second exit, through which the animal would probably escape.

Half an hour later, the hunters returned to the village, they had not captured any prey, however they did not seem upset.

Mostaggeda wielded the spear trying to get used to its weight; it was a pleasant sense of power. He made several moves, fighting an imaginary enemy; he stabbed several times in the air.

He had gone away from the village carrying the spear he had taken from Melemana, taking advantage of an oversight, because the man was absorbed in the preparation of that night's party.

The young man soon got tired of the spear, he found it too heavy. Leaving the gun to one side, Mostaggeda extracted from the leather bag hanging from his shoulder, two strips of leather, with a wider part in the middle. He lifted a round stone, placed it between the leather strips and spun it with speed until one of its extremities was released. The stone was thrown quickly and hit a palm tree, about seven meters away. Mostaggeda smiled satisfied.

That was his greatest secret; he would never reveal it to anyone, not even Menuttaui. A year ago the young man had made friends with a woman, captured in the eastern lands, near the Two Rivers, after the Great Desert. The woman used

to relate that the hunters of her village did with this weapon, which was easy to manufacture.
- Those bastards - The woman smiled when she remembered - they pay dearly every time they attack our people - The slave let out a bitter laugh, despising her captors.
-Our warriors hunt them like birds.
The young Mostaggeda listened attentively to those stories from distant lands, completely different from the world he knew.
The slave died some time later, since then the young man practiced with the slingshot hiding from indiscreet glances. In his youthful innocence he assumed that the sling would help him to become the best hunter of the clan, conquering the respect of the warriors, mainly his father.
He was already able to throw stones at a distance of forty meters, but he still lacked precision, he was only able to hit his targets at less than ten meters, he needed to improve. For half an hour he practiced with the sling. Feeling thirsty, he collected some dates and returned to the village.
Upon reaching the hut, he suddenly came face to face with his father, who seemed furious. Melemana looked fiercely at the spear the young man carried.
-My spear, who allowed you to take it?
Without waiting for an answer, the man dropped a violent blow on the boy's face, which fell backwards, releasing the spear. Melemana kicked strongly on the side of Mostaggeda, which screamed in pain, but the man was still not satisfied, held the young man by the hair to lift him, with his fist firmly closed he hit a punch in the jaw of his son, who collapsed unconscious. At that moment Mashda arrived carrying a large basket of fish, witnessing his fallen son he lunged towards Melemana.
-Nooo, my son! - He tried to push the man away from the boy's motionless body.
Melemana's reaction was instinctive and deadly. Furious, he beat the woman violently, she fell backwards, hitting her head against the rock that was used as a seat, in front of the hut. Mashda shuddered for a brief moment, and then finally stood still. A thread of blood flowed from her head, forming a small puddle in the earth.
Some warriors watched without approach.
Melemana seemed to awaken from his madness, watched his son recovering his senses, then looked at his wife, to finally interrogate with his gaze the warriors who remained distant. From his hut, Susuda made a brief gesture of approval in Melemana's direction and disappeared inside. Melemana bowed to raise her spear. Leaning on it, appearing to control the situation, he pointed his free hand towards the woman's inert body:
- Mostaggeda, removes that corpse from here!

He stepped quickly into the hut and collapsed on the bed, covering his eyes with both hands. Little by little he assimilated all the tragedy that happened in a few minutes.
Mostaggeda was still stunned, one hand holding his jaw, he spat blood shaking his head. When he tried to get up, as he looked towards the hut he discovered Mashda's inert body, he lunged at the woman.
He shouted desperately, hugging his mother's body, several boys, also sons of slaves, approached. After pushing Mostaggeda away with great effort, they moved the woman's body to the place reserved for burying slaves, a short distance from the village. Menuttaui accompanied Mostaggeda, the boy had a swollen face, he still spit blood from time to time, and his friends accompanied him to the lagoon to clean his wounds.
- My mother, the bastard killed her and nobody did anything to stop it!
- You can't go back to your hut, he'll kill you too!
-Fear not, Mostaggeda, together we will help you to build a hut far from your father!
- No, that's impossible, he'll never allow it.
-What do you intend to do, do you plan to flee?
The young man immersed his head for a moment in the water, as he stood up, the liquid ran through his hair to fall back into the lake; he looked at the village with a hateful gaze.
-There is only one way out...
He didn't complete the sentence, but everyone guessed its meaning.

A huge full moon shone when the captives were executed. Their skinned bodies were impaled over the bonfire; the feast of the Red-Haired Men began. No one seemed to remember the incident a few hours ago, for those wild warriors; a clan man had simply executed his slave and administered a lesson to his bastard son. It was nothing out of the ordinary.
- I would have done the same thing - Said one who Melemana could not identify in the group around him, he had the strange feeling that everyone treated him differently, with some respect; everyone had definitely approved of his attitude. About fifteen men sat on stones or directly on the ground, appreciating the fermented drink they removed from a large sea turtle shell, using snails, animal horns, or rustic vessels of dry mud. Within a few minutes the first symptoms of drunkenness manifested themselves, those warriors seemed to have lost their somber character, everyone chatted animatedly, boasted and laughed spectacularly as they drank. In front of the bonfire, two human bodies began to drip abundant fat, which squeaked on contact with the embers, and the penetrating smell of roasted human flesh spread throughout the village.
Sitting with the group, Melemana drank, apparently had completely forgotten the murder. At one point, Agga, who had drunk very little, despite behaving as if

intoxicated, glanced briefly at Susuda. Both observed each other without saying a word, Susuda understood the order. Staggering, the warrior rose, zigzagging toward his hut.

Arriving in front of the entrance he did not stop, without looking back he contoured the hut disappearing from the group's view. Immediately his drunkenness vanished.

He walked steadily and quickly through the shadows to the last hut. His body appeared for a moment in the moonlight, it was the combined sign, from the shadows four warriors armed with stone mallets stood out. Without saying anything the group exchanged glances, with brief gestures of approval, and separated.

Each knew what he should do.

At some distance, lying on the white sand on the shores of the lake, Mostaggeda listened to the laughter and bragging of the warriors gathered around the bonfire. He knew that all of them would soon be drunk and that his father would be with the group, feeding on human flesh. All would be armed only with their daggers, necessary to cut the flesh.

No warrior could participate in a banquet armed with his spear that was the usual rule.

The young man knew that there would be no guards in the village that night, as at previous banquets and rituals. That would be essential to what he intended to do that night.

Those who did not belong to Agga's group of trusted hunters would remain in their huts sleeping.

To avoid sleep, the young man immersed his head in the cool waters of the lake.
-I have to wait; soon everyone will be so drunk that they won't be able to take a step.

Going with caution, Mostaggeda could distinguish the light of the bonfire and the silhouettes of the group, the young man could not identify Melemana, but without a doubt he would be there, he had always strived to conquer Susuda's sympathies.

By midnight, the laughter had ceased. The macabre supper had been consumed, many men were fallen everywhere, completely drunk. Hardly Agga and his henchmen were still seated, conversing quietly. Mostaggeda slipped quickly to Melemana's hut, checking that it was empty.

At the side of the bed he found the spear. With quick movements the boy took a bladder with water, an obsidian knife, the sling and some stones that he had kept under the bed, placed everything inside a bag that he hung on his shoulder and with the wielded spear he left the hut.

At that moment, from a nearby hut there was clearly a drowned out cry and the dull sound of a falling body. A frightened slave emerged screaming from Puanuna's hut. That seemed to unleash a wave of violence; Mostaggeda heard sharp fighting sounds from several huts.

It was when Mostaggeda noticed that Menuttaui left the hut running, while inside there were screams of pain, he seemed to recognize the voice of the chief Turahena. The young woman walked a short distance from her friend without seeing him.

At the entrance to the hut a warrior from Agga's group emerged, holding a blood-stained stone mace. A little further, the warrior Dabagha staggered, his hands holding his belly firmly, from which abundant blood flowed. A shadow lunged over the wounded man to strike him hard on the head.

Indifferent to the drama around him, Mostaggeda ran in the direction of the clarity of the bonfire, in the confusion of the moment no one observed him. As he approached he could first see Susuda and Agga, who were standing in front of the fire, seemed to be waiting for something, they were accompanied by two warriors. A little further back, Mostaggeda saw his father. All remained attentive to what was happening in the huts; several men had left their homes wielding weapons after hearing the screams and signs of struggle. No one paid attention to the shadow that ran wielding a spear toward the campfire.

Susuda was the first to discover the young man when he was already with them. Mostaggeda, seven meters away from his father, stopped and with a strong impulse threw the heavy spear, shouting:

-Melemana!

The man turned the moment the spear hit him in the chest, piercing his body. With an expression of absolute surprise, Melemana stood there, his eyes fixed on the stick that seemed to have sprung from his body. He tried to take a step before collapsing inert to one side. He agonized for a few minutes, enveloped in violent riles, until he died.

Mostaggeda wasted no time; he had calculated everything in detail. His father was still standing when the young man had already turned around to run into the shadows, apparently heading for the north exit. The young man found that no sentries had indeed been placed that night. Leaving behind the set of huts he described a detour, circling the village to run fast towards the hills to the south. At the very moment he was running he heard Menuttaui's voice calling from the shadow of the palm trees. As her friend approached, the young woman sobbed:

- Mostaggeda, Turahena has been murdered!

The girl had apparently missed the best part of the party, thought Mostaggeda as he grabbed her by the arm.

-Run!

They couldn't waste time, the young man knew she would delay him, but he was confident that it would be some time before they started the chase.

In the village, Agga was informed that the chief Turahena and his trusted warriors had been eliminated. That could not have gone better; Melemana's murder gave him the opportunity to deflect suspicions of the massacre by blaming the young Mostaggeda and a supposed group of conspirators, sons of slaves. He approached Susuda and quietly announced.
-A group of bastards murdered Turahena and the rest, Mostaggeda is the leader of the conspiracy.
Susuda made a brief gesture of approval, smiling sarcastically.
The warrior glanced at Melemana's body, which lay in the middle of a large pool of blood.
-Who would have thought, Melemana, after all, you were finally of great use to us.
Agga discreetly dispatched two warriors to capture the young fugitive. At the light of the bonfire he raised both arms in a solemn attitude, preparing to communicate to the clan his version of what had happened that night.

RESCUE

Hor descended from the hills into the great lake. He walked for four days until he reached the margin. That night he camped by the lake, to examine the territory trying to identify the light of bonfires. He discovered no sign; apparently the village of the Red-haired Men was still far to the north.
Anyway, he refrained from lighting a fire, feeding on dried meat.
Before dawn he set out, circling the lake, he walked all morning. In the afternoon he noticed that the lake narrowed, forming a natural channel that stretched for many miles to flow into another lake far to the north. He continued his march, accompanying the water course, finding no signs of human life. At dusk on the second day, he reached the margin of the second lake, proving that its size was even larger than the previous one. The opposite margin was not visible on the horizon.
It moved for two hours, always around the lake.
Then finally, after having ventured into that unknown territory for seven days, that night he observed the light of bonfires at a certain distance.
An hour before dawn Hor restarted the march, walking cautiously until he reached a rocky hill, covered by abundant palm trees and bushes.
From the top he saw the territory in front of him.
To his left the surface of the lake was confused at a distance with the pale clarity of the sunrise; at the bottom, beside the lake, a group of huts stood adjoining a large rock wall. The vast plain was interrupted by isolated forests of palm trees and shrubs. From time to time a hill broke the monotony of the landscape.
Down there, a few kilometres after the village, a group of men and women collected vegetables and grains from the plain.

Forcing his eyesight, he seemed to distinguish the characteristic silhouettes of the Red Hair warriors, along with what seemed to be women collecting seeds.
Hor remained in that place, protected by the shadows of the trees, awaiting the arrival of night to approach the village. He fed on dates and the pulp of some cactus, because his reserves of dried meat were finished.
Among the trees swarmed a great variety of birds and small mammals, but it would be suicide to light a bonfire.
Finally it got dark, it was a clear night, and a huge full Moon illuminated the landscape. Hor walked for an hour until he reached a small stony elevation with little vegetation, a little less than a kilometer from the village. The young man was unaware that the Red-Haired Man did not own dogs, yet he knew that the powerful sense of smell of those men could easily locate him if he was neglected. He observed the direction of the wind, taking all possible precautions before leaning out on top of the hill. He clearly distinguished a great bonfire and some silhouettes circulating around the place, despite the late hour.
He decided to approach the village when everyone was asleep, and prepared to wait. The hours passed and those people were still active, the young man assumed that some kind of ceremony would be taking place. He was thinking of retiring and returning the next night, when he seemed to hear a scream in the distance.
In the village the activity had increased, he saw some people running near the bonfire, he could not understand what it was, but all that could not be a normal situation, something was happening.
Then the moonlight revealed two figures running in his direction, apparently they had just left the village.

Mostaggeda and Menuttaui ran a long way. The girl looked exhausted, so they stopped for a moment.
-Listen, we're going to turn towards that hill, they won't take long to find our footprints, even though they're drunk.
The warriors sent by Agga left the village towards the south, following in Mostaggeda's footsteps. Like the entire Agga's group, they also refrained from drinking and were in perfect condition.
The moon light clearly revealed the path followed by the young man, immediately understood the stratagem of Mostaggeda, accompanying the curve that the young man described around the village. With a fast pace, but barely trotting to save energy, the warriors made their way south. They were veterans of countless hunts and raids, and did not delay in distinguishing the couple, some five hundred meters ahead. Running under the moonlight, they seemed to be heading for the rocky elevation a little further ahead.

Menuttaui ran trying to accompany Mostaggeda's longest steps. Looking back, the girl did not contain a drowned moan when she saw the silhouettes of her pursuers. With a quick glance the young man understood that it would be useless to try to escape, he searched around, the only possible shelter was offered by a pair of palm trees about fifty meters to his right.
-Run to the rocks, I'll try to stop them here- exclaimed the young man as he grabbed the sling, placing a heavy stone between the leather strips.
The two warriors watched the young woman heading for a hill, without speaking, both advanced towards Mostaggeda, which seemed to be trying to hide behind the trunk of two palm trees. The young man turned the sling sharply, throwing a stone that passed with a loud buzzing sound a short distance from the heads of his enemies.
The hunters stopped for a moment, surprised by the unusual force with which the stone had been thrown.
 They exchanged a funny look, before the unexpected weapon, without speaking they separated to escape of possible new stones, approaching the boy.
Mostaggeda left his precarious refuge to launch a desperate race to the hill, Menuttaui ascended to the top, looking back at each step.
The warriors trotted calmly in the direction of the boy who reached the base of the hill, he would be an easy prey.
At that instant the warrior furthest ahead stopped, screaming in pain as a mysterious arrow was buried in his chest. It took him a few seconds to understand that that fine rod was stealing his life. He lifted his head in search of where the arrow came from. Another cry of pain caught his attention, to his rear. As the warrior turned he saw his companion holding the belly and his spear fell to the ground.
Mostaggeda did not understand what was happening, his enemies had stopped, and screamed in pain. The dim moonlight did not allow him to see the arrows, but he could clearly hear the hum of a third arrow crossing the air before submerging into the body of the first warrior with a thud.
The man, with two arrows in his chest, tried to escape, turning around, but could only take two steps before collapsing. His companion tore the arrow from his belly with a roar of rage, looking furiously for the place where his spear had fallen. Mostaggeda did not waste the opportunity, he ran to approach the warrior a little less than ten meters away, turning the sling. The heavy stone produced a loud crack as it impacted the guy's head, which fell to the ground.
It was all over.
Menuttaui approached her runaway companion, looking worried around.
-Are you hurt?
-No, I'm fine, and you?
-What was that, who helped us?

They both heard the sound of footsteps, someone coming down the hill.
The girl looked up. Under the moonlight, there, less than twenty meters away, was Hor.
The young woman let out a scream of surprise; recognizing her, Hor lunged in her direction.
They stood there, embraced in the light of the Full Moon, the girl sobbed. At that moment Hor spotted Mostaggeda going up the hill, he quickly pulled the girl away to prepare the bow.
-No! He's not one of them, he's my friend!
Hor looked suspiciously at Mostaggeda's hair and characteristics, but at the insistence of Menuttaui, who stood in front of his bow, the young man lowered his weapon.
They knew that they could not waste time, without uttering a word they began the march southward.
They walked all night. Hor covered the girl's body with the skin of the leopard he had hunted some time ago. At dawn, after verifying that they were not followed, they decided to camp in an isolated little forest in the middle of the plain, where a herd of gazelles, horses and antelopes grazed.
They lacked food; Hor knew they would need to prepare for the long journey, so he shouted happily when he shot down a gazelle with an accurate arrow shot.
Discarding every precaution, they lit a bonfire to scare away eventual carnivores. Menuttaui slept all morning, completely exhausted.
The boys took advantage of the pause to tell their respective stories, while they prepared the meat of the prey.
A feeling of trust was being born between them.
- You mean Red-Haired Men can't generate daughters, only male sons?
- At least that's what I've seen since I was born.
They both shared a meal, after reserving a good portion for the girl. Some of the meat was arranged to dry on the stones, Mostaggeda shook his head, smiling:
-So you are Hor, I have heard that name many times.
-Yes? - The young redhead gestured towards the young woman, and Hor smiled.
- It seems that you will be forced to hear my name even more, because you will have to come with us.
- I planned to go to the Great River - Mostaggeda pointed to the west.
-As you wish, you are free to do so. With us, however, you could rest for as long as you wish. My clan is small, only a handful of survivors, yet our land is rich in food and resources, you will be welcome.
Shortly afterwards Menuttaui awoke. While he was feeding, Hor told him that his little brother Gen and his father were well, that there were still survivors in the cavern. The young woman was worried about the future:
-They will attack us again, I know. The night we escaped, the old chief was killed.

-Yes, many differences were resolved that night- whispered Mostaggeda enigmatically, without going into details. The young woman looked at him for a moment.
- We are both doomed if we were captured - Menuttaui hugged Hor - They know where our cavern is, we will not be safe there!
Hor understood that the girl was right; he didn't want to lose her again.
-We will stay in the cave long enough to warn our brothers, and then I think we can head for the Great River, as Mostaggeda pretends.
-The Great River is the only place where the men of Agga will not be able to reach us.
They had come to an agreement, and shortly afterwards they continued their march.
They always walked south for more than ten days, until finally they saw the familiar landscape of the rocky wall and the entrance to the cave.
A column of smoke indicated that the cavern was inhabited.

The reunion of the girl with her father and little brother was exciting; the young woman had the painful task of informing them about the death of her mother.
They recounted the adventure as they regained strength, drinking and feeding after the long journey. The cave was well stocked, Serqui had organized everything admirably, the two hunters and the little Gen had worked intensely during all the time Hor was away.
Mostaggeda was greeted with some misgivings at first, though he soon won everyone's trust. The exchange of knowledge was interesting; the young man was surprised at the deadly effectiveness of those light assegais thrown with a propellant, while the members of the clan marveled at the slingshot of the young redhead, who improved his aim every day. Mostaggeda had never approached dogs, he liked the way the animals helped during the hunts or watching the cavern. Menuttaui learned several different techniques for cooking food, as well as the consumption of some vegetables unknown to the mountaineers.
Everyone was happy to meet their family and friends again, so what was originally planned as a quick two-day stage turned into a week of rest.
On the third day, when the whole group was gathered eating the tasty meat of a mountain goat, Mostaggeda presented them with an unknown object, it seemed to be a simple bird's bone with some holes. They had a pleasant surprise when the boy took the little bone to his mouth to sing a soft melody with the flute, the sound multiplied as it echoed inside the cavern.
Everyone listened to him enjoying the melody, at the end, the young redhead explained:

In reality this is not the work of my father's people, my mother taught me, from a distant clan east of the Two Great Rivers, many days' journey from the village of the Red-Haired Men.

At first Hor encountered some resistance from the clan who did not want to leave that territory, mainly because of the welfare provided by the relative abundance of resources.

But they had to face reality, their clan was not numerous, and the enemy knew their location. Finally everyone understood that if they remained in the cavern, sooner or later they would have to face a new attack. The time had come to emigrate and the group began preparations to move to the Great River.

BATTLE IN THE GREAT RIVER

Agga, standing on a platform raised with logs and skins, gazed at his men gathered around him in the center of the village. Susuda, in front of his warriors, with his face painted with ochre tincture, lifted his heavy spear to ovate the new chieftain.

The day after Turahena death, the new leader had been proclaimed by his men. He immediately sent messengers to neighboring villages, communicating the cacique's assassination by a group of enemy looters. Agga offered women and a rich booty for the clans to help him fight the enemy, sending warriors to participate in an incursion against the peoples of the Great River, responsible for the attack on their village. The new cacique promised wealth and land to his allies, after conquering the Great River.

On the other hand Susuda obtained the alliance of the fishing clans of the coast, belonging to the same race. The plan was very simple: to transport with the great canoes of the fishermen a great force by the sea, until the region of the delta, to punish the enemies plundering the villages of the region.

Now standing on the platform, surrounded by a crowd of about one hundred and twenty Red Hair warriors, Agga felt powerful and his eyes shone as he contemplated that horde acclaiming his name.

-The enemy has dared to invade our lands, it must be punished- He exclaimed pretending a great indignation - They know that the gods do not send daughters for our race, they think we are weakened and have dared to attack us. Now they hide behind their sacred river, feeling safe from our vengeance- He paused briefly, clenching his right fist in a gesture of intense hatred. -Yesterday was our village, tomorrow your huts will be destroyed, and that must end!

-We must attack!- shouted Susuda, his companions supported him with angry cries, all lifted their spears, crying out for revenge.

- Friends, at this moment our brothers await us on the beaches of the great sea- he pointed with his ivory spear to the west- Their boats are now ready to transport us to the Great River!

Some warriors were not enthusiastic about a naval campaign; the Red-Haired Men were generally not good swimmers, which is why they avoided sailing. Susuda decided to encourage them by declaring enthusiastically:
-A journey that would take ten days by land, we will complete in just two days by sea. We should only walk half a day to the beach, brothers!
Agga raised both clenched fists, his expression reflecting all his determination:
-War, brothers, war! In two days we will have many slaves and the greatest booty that has ever been conquered!
A furious battle cry rose from the group.
That same day, Agga and his army set out for the Mediterranean coasts.
They walked for two hours to the south, where they wad the lake and then headed for the sea shores. They were armed with spears, stone clubs, wooden clubs with huge stones at the end, and heavy obsidian knives. Some had painted their faces with ochre ink, adorning their heads with feathers of vultures and eagles. They carried bladders with water, and huge pieces of salted meat hanging from sticks.
Agga maintained a reserve of twenty warriors to take care of the village.
When they reached the coast, some fifteen log canoes awaited them; they were solid boats that could face the sea waters transporting up to ten warriors each. A contingent of about twenty-five men joined the main group on the beach. Agga was satisfied, finally realizing his dream of uniting the different clans to annihilate the peoples of the Great River. Previous raids had failed in that swampy land, due to the reduced number of attackers. Now it would be different, never before had such a large force gathered.
By a strange coincidence, on the same day that Agga sailed with his army to the Great River, far away from there, Hor and his small clan began their journey to the same destination, walking through the desert in a march that would take six or seven days.
The fleet sailed for two days, not far from the coast, facing a sea of calm waters.

At dawn on the third day they landed on an arm of the Great River delta.
Agga did not know the delta region, so he immediately sent some explorers to recognize the surroundings, one of them, aboard a fast canoe, should go into the eastern arm of the river, exploring the neighboring territories. Shortly after noon the first explorers returned.
As Agga supposed, there was hardly a village in the delta, it was an old enemy of the Red-Haired men, who had rejected their parents' attack long ago. Hearing the explorers describing the village of the Snail Eaters, Agga saw that it might be a fearsome adversary; by her side, Susuda seemed to doubt the campaign for the first time.
-The population of the village is enormous; it will not be an easy prey.

-I know, but we have the surprise factor, if we attack immediately they won't have time to organize.
Susuda didn't seem very enthusiastic about the idea.
-The canoes in that village are reed, lighter and faster than ours, they could block our retreat.
-Let us guard the explorers of the river; we still don't know what exists on the other side of the Delta.
The last group of explorers returned the next day and was immediately interrogated by Agga, who was visibly anxious.
-There is only one way upstream, and it crosses in front of the village.
-Have they seen you?
-Yes, our canoe caught the attention of some groups of fishermen, and as we passed in front of the village, many people watched us.
-Damn it! - Exclaimed Susuda- They will soon send explorers and discover our presence here.
-But no one harassed us; they barely watched us from the margin, curious.
-What is south of the village?
-We can go into the delta until we reach the main channel of the river, where there are several fishing villages, weakly defended.
Agga and Susuda considered the advantages of eliminating neighboring communities first, before marching against the main village. That action would deprive Ziuzu of the help of his neighbors, while they could establish a base south of the enemy.
-As we sail in front of the village, we will show all our strength.
-That's right, when surrounded, many may leave the village.
-These people are just a group of fishermen and snail eaters, they are not warriors!
-And they will not be able to defeat our men!
Agga and Susuda stared at each other for a moment. They had regained confidence; it would be an easy victory.
At midday the fleet sailed defiantly along the river arm, in front of the village of the Snail Eaters. Ziuzu had been informed that morning of the invader's presence and the village had closed, ready to fight behind its defenses.
From the bamboo parapet, Ziuzu gazed at those Red-Haired warriors, who were making threats aboard their canoes. He could see that the enemy had no bows; as it had always been, the red-haired men continued to rely on the brute force of their rustic spears.
The defenders responded to the cries of the enemy with a thunderous laughter at the sight of their rustic weaponry.
The fat chieftain scratched his jaw with two fingers as he carefully examined the fleet of canoes, finally failing to hide a smile.

- They are very numerous, but do not know the region - He turned to the warriors who accompanied him on the stockade.
-Their weapons are not good, they trust only their number.
When one of his warriors was about to use his bow, the chieftain stopped him.
-No, it's better not to reveal our power until the right moment, my friends.
A plan matured in his mind, as enemy canoes sailed up the delta channel.
Ziuzu was worried that he wouldn't be able to alert the villages upstream.
- The enemy sails along the main arm of the river, if we send messengers through other channels of the delta, they would never arrive in time.
-And by land, through the swamp, it would be impossible.
Someone murmured behind the chief's back:
-They will attack our friends by surprise.

The village of Erihen had ceased to be a simple settlement; about twenty circular huts had been built on the hill. In those months the clan had incorporated several groups of immigrants from different origins. A strong palisade of logs was being erected, yet there were still unfinished sectors.
A small pier was used for the landing of fishermen and merchants who from time to time appeared with their products. The friendly attitude of the village allowed a fruitful communication with distant people, inhabitants of the south of the Great River.
A magnificent wooden altar, illuminated with torches lit every night, projected its light to the opposite bank of the river, becoming a reference for night sailors. It was the place of adoration of the Goddess of Mother Earth, adopted even by some neighboring villages that frequently paid homage to her with offerings. There were still millennia left for the unification of the country that one day would be called Egypt, but commerce and religion already announced this destiny.
That morning a group of fishermen disembarked and asked to speak with Erihen, who immediately attended them:
-Erihen, we need your help, we lost several of our fishermen.
-What happened, Tungo?
The black fisherman, wearing a tunic of braided reeds at his waist, he explained:
-The demons have sent a mad hippopotamus, which attacks our canoes killing their occupants. For some unknown reason, his behavior is more aggressive than usual.
Another fisherman intervened:
-The beast arises under the canoes without giving time to escape, overturns the boats and attacks the castaways.
-What can I do to help? - Erihen was interested.
- We know the fearsome power of the small arrows of your warriors.
-Do you think our arrows will be enough to end that threat?

- We have tried to kill him with our spears, without obtaining results, neither the arrows of our neighbors managed to rid us of that demon.

Erihen turned to Nungal, who stood beside him listening in silence.

-What do you think?

-I think we can solve that problem if the animal shows its body for a few seconds.

-Who will go? -Asked Erihen, although he already knew the answer, so he smiled as he listened to his friend.

Nungal shrugged, carefree, as the giant Mumny approached.

-I'll go too; I've been too idle these days.

The fishermen deposited four huge fish on the altar of Goddess Earth, thanking for the help.

Nungal and Mumny left with the fishermen an hour later.

As they said goodbye, Nungal greeted them shouting from the canoe:

-With a bit of luck, we'll be back tomorrow!

- We'll bring hippopotamus for lunch- completed Mumny as he lay down in the middle of the canoe, one leg out of the gunwale.

It was getting dark and everything seemed to be calm in that village. Agga knew that enemy dogs could ruin the surprise factor of the attack. That is why he stopped the fleet at a safe distance. Agga's boat moved forward to the bend in the river, from where he could see the small village at the top of a small hill. The light of several torches flashed in the waters, allowing everything to be examined in detail.

Its inhabitants, mostly black skinned, did not inspire fear. Susuna muttered:

-I see many women.

Agga turned to Zukanna, the warrior who was in a canoe a little further back.

-You sail with four warriors, greet friendly to whoever is watching you and continue upstream until you leave the field of vision, then disembark and return immediately, you must start the attack from that side. After you have started, the main group will attack directly, after disembarking at the pier.

He turned to Susuda, who waited in silence.

- You must disembark with twenty warriors before the river bend and you will attack the village by land from this side, while Zukanna does it from the opposite side.

Without uttering a word, Susuna took immediate action, gathering her group.

As Zukanna moved away, Agga insisted, clenched his fist tightly.

-Don't be late; we will attack after you have started!

Zukanna nodded slightly, rowing vigorously down the middle of the river.

Old Kutum argued amicably with two businessmen, who offered him some brightly colored stones from the Southern Country, as well as elephant tusks, chunks of bananas and some medicinal herbs. With a flint knife he made marks on a baboon bone, counting the goods offered. That bone would then be compared with the marks that the merchants would make on a similar bone when inspecting the merchandise offered by the village. It was a simple and fair system for closing good deals, used millennia before the invention of writing.
Kutum turned to contemplate a canoe that at that moment passed in front of the wharf, sailing quickly by the center of the river, some of its crew raised an arm saluting in silence.
The three merchants responded to the greeting, Kutum frowned.
-Strange people, do you know them?
The businessmen shrugged, one of them commented:
-They seemed to be people from other lands; I've never seen a canoe like that on the river.
-It's getting dark, why would they want to risk sailing upriver at night?
Kutum knew that it would be normal to camp in the village until the next day, but a canoe with five people didn't seem to represent a threat, so he decided to forget the matter, turning his attention to business.
-Look, I will never consider these bananas with the same value as my medicines...
Considered out of sight of the villagers, Zukanna landed. The warriors placed the canoe out of the water, and rushed quickly to the village, without worrying about silencing the march, they wanted to draw attention.
The monotony of that late afternoon was suddenly broken by those five warriors who suddenly emerged from the vegetation, uttering furious cries.
A man carrying a log for the palisade fell through with a spear strike. Other workers leapt from the trees and ran towards the village shouting cries of alarm. Kutum and the merchants were stunned for a moment, until the old man reacted.
-You get in your canoes before it's too late!
Immediately he ran up the hillside to the huts, Erihen already showed up accompanied by four warriors with their deadly bows ready. Several women took refuge with their children in the huts. The chieftain and his warriors headed for the part of the palisade that was not yet finished, that would be the vulnerable spot that should be protected.
Erihen attacked immediately, the small arrow stuck into the side of the most advanced warrior. The guy still advanced four steps, staggered and fell, abundant foam gushed from his mouth. Zukanna was running after the wounded man, and for a moment he did not understand what was happening, how an insignificant arrow could kill so quickly?
At his side, two other warriors succumbed quickly.

The two survivors turned, terrified, what strange power did those people have? At that moment a loud noise was heard indicating that the fighting had begun on the opposite side.

Susuda's largest group attacked noisily, killing several people in that sector. Erihen and his warriors turned to the new threat, responding to the enemy with their deadly arrows. At first four warriors fell, Susuda understood the deadly power of the archers, and ordered a direct attack on the four individuals. From the palisade several warriors joined in defense, using assegais thrown from a great distance with propellers.

Two dogs shot down an attacker ahead of the group, crossing the palisade. A blow from a mace liquidated the invader. As Erihen was retreating back to the palisade, Agga's group disembarked. The esplanade in front of the village was suddenly replete with Red-haired warriors who advanced wielding their heavy weapons. From the other side, Zukanna and her companion regained their courage as they saw their entire clan invading the village, and turned around to attack. The siege was complete; the defenders began to fall, despite causing many casualties to the enemy.

From the palisade, Erihen concentrated on the invaders of the esplanade, whom he kept in line with his arrows, when he was mortally wounded in the back by Zukanna's spear. The redheaded warrior and his companion had managed to approach the group from the rear, at a short distance the bows were useless and all were slaughtered. The last archer received a deadly blow to the head.

The massacre began, for the defenders all was lost.

As his men liquidated the last defenders, Susuda examined the small arrow that had so bluntly eliminated his warriors. Zukanna, who witnessed the deadly effects of those arrows up close, ran a hand over her face, covered with intense sweat.

-Men who generally endure terrible wounds without retreating today were struck by a single arrow, which only slightly wounded some in one arm.

-That's right, I've seen them die of minor wounds, I don't understand that power, and they're arrows of the devil! - Susuda, who had never faced poisoned arrows, was surprised.

With cautious gestures he examined the red feathers that stood out on each small pole.

Unaware of all that was happening around him, Agga gazed in admiration at the statue of the Earth Goddess, imagining what she would look like in her own village. The fighting was over and the first columns of smoke were rising. In the destroyed village one could hardly hear the crying of some children and the lament of the captured women.

That morning Hor and his companions finally arrived at the village of the Dining Room of Caracoles; it had just dawned but the village already seemed to be in full activity, the atmosphere was tense, the travelers noticed the preparations for war.
When arriving at the bridge the guardian informed them that the village would be attacked at any moment, all those who were in the enclosure should collaborate in their defense. When asked who the enemy was, the answer surprised them:
-They are warriors with white skin and reddish hair, coming from an unknown land. At that moment he looked at Mostaggeda - They are just like him - in a quick movement he lifted the spear.
Hor interceded:
- Don't be fooled by appearances, warrior, this man is our friend and we have come to help.
The guard seemed to be confused, looking for the help of his companion, who had remained silent a little further back. Hor stepped forward:
-We know this enemy well; we know where they come from!
On hearing that, the guard signaled the warriors at the other end of the bridge, and authorized the entry of Hor, Mostaggeda and Menuttaui, who had to surrender their weapons in order to cross.
-Our chief will certainly want to talk to you, hurry!
When the group was in the middle of the bridge, little Gen ran towards his sister, dodging the guard who tried to stop him. The second guardian intervened.
- Leave it, it's just a child - He gestured to the group that had stopped, Gen already reached them, standing behind Menuttaui.
The group was led to the presence of Ziuzu, who was coordinating the defenses. From the first moment his cunning eyes were fixed on Mostaggeda, examining his reddish hair. Hor stepped forward, placing his arm on the boy's shoulders.
-Sir, this is a long story, but it will suffice for the moment to say that we owe our lives to this young man, who was a slave of the enemy - he paused, bowing his head with respect - My name is Hor, the clan that was ruled by my father was slaughtered by these people. They have their village far to the east, in the great lakes.
-What are you looking for here at this moment?
-We left our land, plundered by those damned warriors of Red Hair; our intention was to take refuge in the Great River.
-You didn't come at a good time.
-We didn't know what was happening; now we want to fight our common enemy. I'm the chief of my clan, I have already fought against the Red-Haired Men and I know how to kill them!
-If you wish to fight then you have arrived in good time, be welcome... and I also know how to kill those demons.

The fat chieftain smiled broadly.
-After the victory we will be able to talk about your refuge in the great river.
-May it be as you wish, sir.
The humility of that young warrior won the confidence of the kind Ziuzu, who decided to reveal his plan to them.
-Yesterday the enemy entered, sailing upriver - He stopped and smiled again - they will only be able to go the same way.
 -How do you intend to prevent them from getting through?
-My archers stand guard, and we have crossed lianas and trunks below the surface of the water, they will not be able to sail through, we will force them to disembark.
-And when they disembark?
-Our village will be closed, it will be impossible for them to get into the swamps, the only way out will be to swim across the river trying to escape by land.
-You'll force them to retreat along the same road we did.
-Mostaggeda intervened for the first time. It's an arid territory, with few water sources.
Hor smiled - It's a difficult journey even for those who are well supplied.
-We cannot forget that Agga knows the territory well, he will manage to escape!
-It's possible, Mostaggeda, but in any case it will be a hell for anyone who ventures out there, as a fugitive.
Menuttaui, taking Gen by the hand, asked Ziuzu.
-His archers are good?
The fat chieftain smiled broadly, shaking the child's hair.
 - They are the best in the world!

It was dawn. Nungal and Mumny sailed down the Great River, back to the village. The grateful fishermen transported him after the help received, both felt satisfied. In a quick hunt they had shot down the hippopotamus, which would now feed the fishermen for a long time.
The gigantic Mumny slept sitting, Nungal by his side gazed at the landscape, a slight fog rose from the surface of the river; from time to time a fish broke the water mirror with a violent pigtail. On the banks, the birds were already greeting the new day with their song, the usual bustle that characterized the fauna of the river seemed to fill everything. On the sand, some crocodiles pretended to sleep, waiting for some animal to approach to drink.
Nungal knew something was wrong when he noticed the smell of smoke over the river. Shortly afterwards he saw the thick black columns rising from the vegetation.
As he turned the last bend of the river, the tragic scene was revealed before his eyes, the village was completely destroyed. Old Kutum had sat on a stone, his

gaze lost at some distant point, he seemed utterly dejected. Beside the old man were some children, a woman crying, and many wounded people.
A long line of corpses had been carefully arranged beneath the trees.
Nungal and his companions disembarked in a leap to run towards Kutum, which on seeing them seemed to react. In a few seconds he informed them of what had happened.
Nungal wasted no time, while Mumny collected a handful of arrows from the warehouse that Erihen wisely ordered to be built in a place excavated behind the huts, Nungal immediately prepared to organize the reconstruction, Kutum listened to his instructions attentively.
-After burying the corpses, and extinguishing the last sources of fire, try to build or repair at least one hut, which will serve as a shelter for the survivors. If you don't get a canoe to get help from the fishermen nearby don't worry, I will bring help from Ziuzu, who possibly was also attacked. One of the fishermen promised to stay in the village to help, while his companion would drive Nungal to the delta, then sail to his village in search of help for reconstruction.
Half an hour later a furious Nungal embarked, armed with his bow and a short propelled spear. As he left, he said goodbye to Kutum and Mumny.
-I promise to bring the statue of the Goddess and raise the altar again!
The old man remained watching the canoe until it disappeared in a bend.
Little by little, groups of fugitives, women and children who took refuge in the surrounding vegetation were returning to the village.

In the village of the snail eaters, a sentry aboard a light canoe of junks and papyrus arrived quickly to jump to land on the esplanade, exclaiming.
- Here they come; there are more than ten canoes! - A warrior hastened to remove the light boat from the river to hide it in the waters of the lake, on the other side of the esplanade.
Everything was ready, Ziuzu watched from the palisade; apparently he was calm and confident, because from time to time he showed his nice smile when he commented something with Hor and Menuttaui, who were next to him. The bridge connecting the stilt houses village with the esplanade had been closed. The esplanade, normally a place full of life, where a multitude worked or walked with fish or fruits, was now deserted; it was about eighty meters wide and barely thirty meters separated the river from the lake. This land had no obstacle that could serve as a refuge for the invaders who eventually managed to disembark. Whoever ventured there would be an easy target for the archers from the palisade. Eighty meters further on began the dense vegetation, where about forty archers hid, the reserve force of Ziuzu, in charge of preventing the enemy's escape to the swamp.

On board her canoe, Agga could not divert the eyes of the wooden goddess, next to her Susuda caught the attention of the chieftain.
-Agga, we're coming to the village.
The day before they had managed to pass, but now the enemy had to be prepared, Agga decided to return by the same road, because the delta was unknown to him, the invaders could become disoriented in that tangled of canals and swamps.
-Don't worry, we'll pass.
They had seized some boats from the plundered village, now they had fifteen canoes, heavily laden with warriors, many women captives and all the product of the plunder. The attack had cost too much, they lost fifteen men because of those mysterious arrows, which made it impossible to organize a base in that place. But Agga was satisfied.
 The whole world would talk about his feat; he was the only warrior of his people who managed to defeat the enemy of the Great River.
The column of canoes sailed slowly, dragged by the gentle current of the river, no one rowed, and everyone grabbed their spears anxiously. Unlike the day before, now no insults were heard from the margin, soon after Susuda could see the enemy village, and immediately drew Agga's attention again.
-They await us, watch the margins.
The defenders already saw the whole column of enemy canoes; a frightening silence reigned in the place. On the palisade, Ziuzu slowly leaned forward.
-Almost... almost... almost....
 At that moment the canoe that was sailing in the first place rose violently, to overturn when it hit a thick submerged trunk. The seven occupants fell into the water and swam trying to cling to the canoe, which was stranded between the obstacles. Ziuzu's loud laughter echoed through the village.
-Take it, you bastards! - And all the inhabitants echoed, laughing and defying the enemy.
The canoes that came behind began to hit each other noisily and against the obstacles, Agga understood the enemy's plan.
-Back, row back, we must retreat!
Only six canoes managed to retreat. Upon discovering that a group of captive women were in the canoes that retreated, Ziuzu exclaimed:
-Attack the others; watch out for the captive women!
The defenders threw a shower of arrows on the rest of the fleet, while in the group that retreated, a canoe escaped up the river, while the remaining five headed towards the opposite margin. The rest of the fleet was trapped between the obstacles, and many warriors were wounded by the defenders, some of whom received up to three arrows but continued to resist, trying to hide between the canoes or under the water. Agga understood that these were different arrows

to those faced the day before. At that moment the Ziuzu reserve group came into action, riddled with arrows the warriors who crew the stranded ships.

Numerous bodies floated inert in the river, and their blood attracted an unexpected ally, some crocodiles rushed on the men who remained in the water. Many of them, terrified, sought salvation on the esplanade, to be slaughtered by the defenders from the palisade.

Agga reacted to the gravity of the situation by ordering the landing on the eastern bank of the river.

Only the crew of five canoes, some forty warriors and seven captive women, left the boats to flee to the prairie, entering the desert.

At that moment the canoe that transported Nungal was moving along the delta channel, unexpectedly emerging from meeting the canoes that were trying to escape the battle. A quick glance was enough for the black warrior to understand the situation, with quick movements he prepared the bow, at the precise moment in which the last canoe able to navigate went up the river. His five crew members rowed frantically with their attention turned to the village behind them. They paid no attention to the solitary enemy at his front, until the first arrow was buried in the shoulder of the first rower. The man fell backwards, shaken to his knees. When they saw the foam sprouting from the wounded man's mouth, terror paralyzed their companions, who recognized the dreaded red feathered arrow. When they tried to react by deflecting the course of the canoe, another arrow took its life. From their position on land, Ziuzu, Hor, Mostaggeda, Menuttaui and the rest of the group witnessed the action of the lone black warrior standing in his canoe, firing his deadly arrows at the enemy. The penultimate man raised his hands high, after throwing his weapons into the river, actually tried to surprise Nungal, because behind his back hid the last warrior, awaiting the moment to throw his spear. Without hesitating, Nungal threw his arrow, right in the throat of the enemy, who after a violent jump fell on the agonizing bodies of his companions. Seeing his play fail, the last enemy threw himself into the water, swimming desperately beneath the surface. Suddenly the river burst into a sudden explosion of water and foam when a huge crocodile captured the fugitive. A large stain of blood rose to the surface, slowly diluting.

The Great River regained its eternal calm.

On the esplanade, several men approached the margins, contemplating the end of the battle. Some of them proceeded to remove several submerged logs, to allow access to the canoe of Nungal, which shortly after disembarked, acclaimed by the warriors.

From the palisades, Ziuzu exclaimed, happy.

-That's what I call victory!

His warriors released an exclamation that crossed the marshy land of the delta in a thousand echoes, proclaiming the victory of the Great River and its inhabitants.

THE COUNTER ATTACK

The group was gathered on the esplanade as some people worked on the bridge installation, all were determined to reorganize life in the village after the fulminant victory. Ziuzu contained the jubilant demonstrations of its people out of respect for the tragedy that would strike its neighbors.
Inside, the chieftain repeated himself again and again, euphoric.
- We defeated the enemy without suffering any loss! Not even a dead man!
That seemed to him an incredible feat.
 Nungal, who had been recognized by all as Erihen's successor, was already giving his first orders for the reconstruction of the village.
-We'll to need help to build new huts and a palisade.
Ziuzu placed an arm on Hor's shoulder.
-Here's a group of brave warriors looking for a place to settle.
Nungal watched Hor and his people.
 -They can settle in the village, they are welcome.
Apparently, that meant submitting to the new leader, the young Hor refrained from mentioning his position as chief of his people, due to the gravity of the moment.
That question would be discussed at the appropriate time.
Nungal organized his arrows into two large bunches that he introduced into the quiver he carried at his waist. Little Gen and his father watched the fragile arrows with attention; Serqui did not hide his admiration.
-Never in my life had I seen such effective arrows.
-When it is all over, I will reveal the secret of our arrows to you, my friends - He turned to Ziuzu - We must seize the opportunity, at this moment the enemy is weakened, fleeing through the desert.
Ziuzu made an affirmative gesture - You can take my best twenty warriors and all the supplies you need!
Hor manifested his willingness to participate.
-I have accounts to settle with Agga, I want to participate!
Mostaggeda, from the corner where he leaned disdainfully on his spear, intervened. -I'll go too. Nungal looked at him with distrust, staring closely at the guy whose appearance resembled his enemies.
- Who are you and what interest do you have in this fight?
Hor interceded on the young man's behalf.
-It was thanks to Mostaggeda that I was able to rescue Menuttaui from slavery, he has conquered our trust.

Mostaggeda commented sarcastically - If you don't want my company, chief, you can stay here because we know the region well and we will know what must be done. Nungal hid his surprise by quietly examining the group of young warriors. After reflecting for a few minutes, he smiled briefly, responding in a calm voice:
- I hope you will accept my company, then.
 The comment ended with the brief discussion, Serqui indicated with the hand towards the quiver, in the waist of Nungal.
-If you did not participate, your arrows would have the obligation to accompany us, cacique.
On the bridge, little Gen was carrying a heavy lance from the Red-Haired Men.
-I want to go too!
 Menuttaui came smiling to help his little brother.
-Gen, I need help to rebuild the village of our new friends, you will not try to abandon me.
The boy expressed his annoyance with an eloquent gesture.
-Work, work, that's all I'm good for... I want to fight!
Dragging with difficulty the heavy spear went towards the lake, in that instant an idea sprouted in his fertile imagination:
 -Maybe I can hunt frogs with this spear.

On that day two groups left the village of the snail eaters: a small fleet of canoes transported a group upstream, destined to help in the reconstruction of the village, and a second larger group was transported to the eastern bank of the river. The army included the twenty Ziuzu warriors, armed with bows, spears and their triangular leather shields, commanded by Taklamakan, the cacique's trusted warrior. They all wore the characteristic skin thongs of their clan. Some carried small bags of reed, carrying provisions of snails preserved in salt. Nungal walked in front of the column, accompanied by Mumny, the tall black warrior with whom he already lived many adventures. Both carried their small bows, and a short propelled spear. A little further back Hor marched, with his large bow, a flint dagger at the waist, a heavy quiver of long arrows at the back, and two very light spears with a bone propeller. He was accompanied by two surviving warriors from his village, similarly armed. At the end of the column Mostaggeda wielded a heavy spear taken from the booty captured in the recent battle, from his waist hung the leather straps of the sling. On his shoulder he carried a small leather bag containing stones. From time to time the young man leaned over to pick up some stone he liked because of its round shapes. Three dogs completed the group. Some warriors of the Ziuzu clan carried long sticks of salted meat, muffled torches and bladders with water, indispensable for the long journey that awaited them.

In front of the group stretched the infinite meadow of red earth, vegetation became scarcer as they moved away from the river.
At a certain moment Nungal stopped, observing the clear trail left by the enemy. Taklamakan, Hor and their two warriors approached:
-It's strange; they don't bother to hide their tracks.
-Let us not forget that they are fleeing, in these conditions these details are neglected, we all know where they are going.
Hor examined the footsteps, clearly distinguished the marks left by the Red-Haired Men and their captives - they know we follow them - Mostaggeda contemplated the footprints -Agga has a lot of experience, he hardly commits carelessness, mainly in the desert.
Hor observed him -What do you suggest? - Nungal also interrogated him with a glance. Mostaggeda passed his hand over a sharp mark on the ground.
-They want us to follow them that are their intention - Taklamakan looked towards the horizon:
- In that case we shouldn't keep them waiting, come on!
Hor hurried his steps to stand next to the black warrior.
-My father paid a very heavy price for despising that enemy.
 With his short spear over his shoulder, Nungal replied.
-Do you think we're making a mistake?
-I'll answer you later; I think I can guess what they're planning!

At that very moment, half a day away, Susuda slapped one of the women who was walking with less energy than the other captives.
-Don't be late, or I'll kill you right here, woman!
The captives didn't understand his language, but the threatening gestures of that corpulent warrior covered with scars left no doubt about his intentions.
The group walked slowly, they were more numerous than their persecutors, although some of those forty men were unarmed, because they had lost their spears as they hurriedly left the canoes.
Two wounded warriors had managed to stag the blood with plasters of herbs and mud, yet they marched with difficulty.
Agga stopped and looked back; Susuda rinsed the sweat from her face with the back of her hand. The wooden statue was placed on the ground and the column of warriors stopped the march.
-They must be following in our footsteps by now.
-We are carrying women, wounded, and looting, I think they will reach us in two or three days.
-You're right, Susuda, and we have little water.
They had some bladders that were insufficient for everyone; Agga analyzed the situation, thoughtful.

-I think we can solve both problems all at once.
Agga pointed to the southeast with the spear.
- Three days away is the river pass, where in the previous raid we ambushed the enemy. If we go there we move away from our destination, but we can get water and prepare an ambush.
Susuda nodded, he had participated in the previous ambush, and however the current enemy possessed weapons that had awakened a superstitious fear inside him. Guessing his thoughts, Agga tried to reassure him.
-The enemy also had bows in that ambush; we should only fight a short distance, as we did that time.
Without worrying about hiding the footprints, the group diverted course for the southeast. In the middle of the column, the women were walking surrounded by their captors, some of them at the edge of their forces.

The column stopped when Nungal made a brief gesture, pointing to the footprints.
-Here they stopped briefly before changing direction.
With a quick glance Hor pointed to the south.
-I knew it, they're heading for the only source of water in the territory.
Nungal pointed east.
-If we continue in this direction, we can go ahead and ambush them.
Hor reflected for a moment, Mostaggeda shook his head, intervening:
-To the east there is no place for a good ambush, and the footprints indicate that they outnumber us.
Nungal looked at the horizon, towards the southeast:
-Does that river offer us any possibility?
Hor murmured enigmatically:
-That's where they plan to kill us all.
Hearing those words, there was silence, Hor continued:
-In that place they ambushed my father and his whole group.
Taklamakan approached:
-Do you think they intend to repeat the ambush?
-I'm sure, but there is something in our favor- he paused briefly, observing his companions- this time they don't know that we know their plans, they think they will take us by surprise.
Nungal expressed his doubts - Aren't we putting ourselves in the wolf's mouth?
-No, on this occasion the advantage will be on our side.
-How far is the river?
-We can camp here until midnight, and then walk to reach the river at dawn.
Nungal observed the position of the sun, it was about two hours before nightfall, he ordered to camp in the place. It was not necessary to hide their presence; the

enemy knew they were there, so they lit a bonfire. The delta warriors distributed some fruits and snails. Sitting a short distance from the campfire, Mumny contemplated a ripe fig Taklamakan offered him.
-The magic fruit.
-Magic, a fig? - Taklamakan was surprised, next to him Nungal smiled, as he ate a piece of dried meat.
-In our village a magic happened that we could all witness, tell them, Mumny.
The giant warrior placed the fig between his teeth, biting slowly.
-In the region of our ancestors there were plenty of fig trees, which are very appreciated by everyone. One day our old sorceress wanted to eat figs, it was the time when they matured, but there was a problem: the trees were a two-hour walk away. At the insistence of the woman, who was much appreciated by the clan, two warriors prepared to make the trip to get some fruits. The next day, to the happiness of the old woman, they returned with abundant figs, even carrying some fig tree branches with various fruits. The old woman tasted several fruits, which she also distributed among the whole group. At some point someone threw the fig tree branches outside the cave, in a place reserved for depositing remains of food, bones and other leftovers from the clan.
Time passed, the old woman died the following winter.
One day, much later, we were surprised to discover that a fig tree had grown in that place, next to the cave. No one understood what magic the old woman had used. From that day on, the clan celebrated that magic venerates the memory of our sorceress, thanks to her we had figs there nearby, it would not be necessary to travel to collect those fruits.
Nungal threw some bush branches into the fire:
-It's as if tomorrow a bush sprouts here, because I've thrown its branches.
-The old woman didn't throw the branches into the fire; she threw them into a corner. Some warriors exchanged sarcastic glances, although nobody said anything.
Mumny raised his right hand - I swear on my ancestors, it's all true.
Hor took the opportunity to talk to Nungal.
-That was a fascinating story, but there's something that interests me even more. He paused for a moment, perhaps constrained by confessing his ignorance - ever since I saw you in action on the river, my curiosity about the arrows you use has been aroused.
Nungal smiled slightly.
-You too? - He turned to his companion with a tired gesture -Explain to them, Mumny.
The black man drew two arrows from his quiver:
-Yellow feather arrows are used for hunting, red feather arrows are reserved for our enemies.
- Why do they kill so quickly?

-The red feather arrows are like snakes, with a simple bite, they kill.
-Then they are poisoned arrows... - Hor was surprised, it was something he had never seen and not even imagined could exist.
- What kind of poison do you use, where do you get it, from snakes? Mumny smiled - It's from a fish.
- A fish?
- Yes, it's a fish that in the summer remains buried under the dry mud, where it can stay up to four or five months, waiting for the new rainy season. If you are unlucky enough to step on the mud where this fish hides, you are lost; the poison is concentrated in the spines of its back.
Nungal completed:
-My people learned to catch this fish without killing it, we extract the poison from its dorsal spines.
Mumny smiled as he saw the surprised expressions of his companions.
 -We boiled that poison with water and in that mixture we bathed the tips of our arrows for an entire night. The yellow feathered arrows have a lighter poison, which is removed with the blood of the hunted animal. That's why we can feed ourselves without taking any risks.
Mumny raised his arm with the little arrow proudly - We have already stopped even lions and jackals with only one arrow.

Around midnight the group set out, the Moon was hidden in the horizon. They walked in silence, protected by the intense darkness. Mostaggeda had insisted on marching to the forefront, his fine sense of smell could prevent the group. His black companions were not very convinced of his abilities, but they did not object.
It was still dark when they peered cautiously over the hill that bordered the river. They had tied the dogs in a bush half an hour ago; they could spoil everything with their barking.

Agga had repeated all the movements of the first ambush, which this time would be in the opposite direction. The group went through the strong current and continued the march up the hill a little further. There remained two warriors taking care of the captives, the rest of the group made a detour to return to the place of the ambush. Disciplined, they were distributed among rocks and trees. Agga and Susuda remained on the bank of the river, hidden among the vegetation. Shortly before dawn Agga noticed that the wind was not favorable, so he decided to highlight a forward-looking observer, who should await the approach of the enemy, one or two kilometers ahead, so he could warn his companions. He was unaware that his pursuers were already there, a short distance behind the hill.

Nungal and Hor had planned an attack from two fronts, taking advantage of the fact that the Snail Eaters were excellent swimmers, accustomed to fluvial activities. Taklamakan selected ten warriors who left immediately, with the objective of crossing to the opposite margin three hundred meters upstream; to return in direction of the local of the ambush, once there they should wait for a signal to attack.

A sentry warned Nungal about a solitary warrior who was heading for the hill at the time, it was the observer sent by Agga. Calculating his direction, they imagined he would pass about forty yards to his right. Mostaggeda warned quietly:

-When he reaches the top of the hill the wind will carry our scent, and he will alert his companions!

Silently Nungal wielded his small bow to slide into the shadows, towards the enemy. The warrior of Red Hair walked with all his attention directed towards the horizon, illuminated by the faint light of dawn. At that moment he stopped abruptly, his body tense. The breeze will reveal to him the human scent nearby. He was trying to locate the origin of the trail when he felt a painful sting in his arm; in the first instant he imagined that it was a scorpion. He understood the terrible truth as he discovered the black warrior behind a bush, his small bow pointed in its direction.

When he perceived the red feather of the arrow sticking out of his arm, he tried to turn back to sound the alarm, but his strength failed him, after two staggering steps he rolled down the slope of the hill. A trace of white foam erupted from his mouth marking the trajectory.

The warrior had not shouted, however the group remained expectant, awaiting some alarm signal from the river.

Everything was in silence.

Although Agga did not yet know, he had just lost the initiative, the ambush turned against him. Three hundred yards up a group of ten warriors had crossed the river and slipped through the shadows in their direction.

Relying on her advanced sentry, Agga neglected himself, imagining that the enemy was still far away.

Susuda inspected the place, walking through the current to examine the positions of his men. Some chewed a piece of dried meat; others had climbed to the rocks to remove their bodies from the water. He came to the opposite bank, walking to the place where there was a group that should allow the enemy to pass and attack him from behind after everyone was inside the river.

Without knowing it, Susuda was revealing the position of his men for the enemy that, from the hill, accompanied all his movements.

Hor discussed with his companions the first steps of the attack:

-We have four enemies on this side of the river, the rest, we don't know how many there will be, they are distributed between the vegetation and the stones along the pass.
Nungal signaled Mumny, who approached.
-We will take care of the first warriors; we already know where they are. If we control the entrance of the pass, our friends can occupy the other bank, capturing the enemy inside the river.
Hor nodded.
-If I'm not fooled, the women are safe a little further ahead, as they did in the previous ambush.
-After defeating them, we must be quick to prevent the guards from killing the women or escaping with them.
Daylight was enough, allowing them to identify several enemies waiting in their positions.
It was time to attack, before the direction of the wind changed and the surprise factor was lost. Nungal and Mumny skillfully slid through the bushes, descending the hillside to within a hundred feet of enemies. With one glance they agreed, they had already selected the first targets.
With an almost imperceptible buzz the fine arrows reached their targets.
The fall of the bodies gave the alarm, the two remaining warriors immediately discovered the enemies who were a short distance away.
Their reactions were completely opposite.
While one of them threw a roar to ram in the direction of Nungal, his companion escaped running through the bushes to jump into the water, shouting:
-The enemy is here!
The warrior who was running towards Nungal was easily stopped by an accurate arrow that pierced his chest. From the hill, Hor could see several warriors ambushed in the center of the river disappearing, alerted by the screams of his companion.
On the other side of the river, the cries of alarm were interpreted as the signal waited by the warriors of Taklamakan, who initiated the attack. Their arrows were not poisoned, but they were also mortally accurate. Agga heard the hum of huge arrows raining down on his companions, and understood that the enemy had already crossed the river.
His plan had failed.
The red-haired chieftain crawled to the margin, signaling to Susuda and several companions. To avoid being surrounded, they decided to leave their position moving among the vegetation until a hundred meters downstream, in that point they undertook a fast race towards the hill. In the pass, the group inside the riverbed, hidden among the rocks, suddenly discovered that it had been surrounded, when Hor's group settled down on the bank of the river to throw

them a shower of arrows. On the opposite bank, another group cut off the exit. The men of Red Hair were not good swimmers, the escape across the river seemed impossible to them.
They succumbed one by one.
A group of seven survivors tried to make their way in a fierce charge against the Snail Eaters warriors. In the brief battle, arrows and spears eliminated the group, some of them armed with simple branches and pieces of trunks.
Arriving on the other side of the hill, Susuda tried violently to stand the group of women tied to each other, kicking and striking them with his spear. Agga arrived at that moment, panting as he looked back with visible concern, fearing to see the enemy group emerge.
-The women will delay our escape; we must get rid of them!
Susuda wielded her flint knife, holding one of the young women by the arm, was about to strike a deadly blow, when the chieftain stopped him:
-Don't kill them; you just have to hurt them, that'll buy us time to get away!
The group set off to the desert, barely twelve warriors remained, Agga had lost twenty-eight men in the river, and it was a real disaster.

Hor and a group of warriors rushed to the hill following the trail of the enemy. Shortly thereafter they found the women, freed them from their bonds and, walking with difficulty, led them to the bank of the river.
Nungal, as Agga supposed, did not immediately launch the chase, and his men inspected the vegetation looking for possible hidden enemies. They spent the rest of the day caring for the wounded. They had lost six warriors, all of them belonging to the group that had crossed the river and had to face the most intense enemy attacks.
Three wounded were not in danger of death; however they could delay the march. Mostaggeda went to look for the dogs, moored a short distance away.
It had been a victory; the enemy group was reduced to a little more than ten men. Hor and Nungal analyzed the situation:
-They don't take much distance, but the women will slow down our march.
-Here they will be safe as well as the wounded warriors.
At that moment Taklamakan approached:
-We have fulfilled our mission, the enemy is defeated, my orders are to return to the delta, with all my warriors.
-I thought your orders were to put an end to those cursed ones.
-They no longer represent a threat, only a handful escaped, and it is my duty to care for the wounded.
-All the wounded women belong to my village, but that won't stop me from going after those murderers!
Taklamakan shook his head, apparently he would not budge.

-I also have several wounded warriors, I will have no trouble transporting the women to your village, but I must follow my orders.
Avoiding an argument with her ally, Nungal weighed the situation for a few minutes -The damned are carrying our Goddess, it's my duty to rescue her.
-It's a ten-day march to the land of the Red-Haired Men - calculated Hor- and it's possible we'll catch up with them sooner.
Nungal seemed determined to leave behind the enemy immediately.
-Who will accompany me?
Without hesitation, Hor replied.
-I will go with you, Nungal; there are still women slaves in the enemy village, women of my own clan.
Mostaggeda stood beside Hor.
-Without my help, you will get nowhere.
Hor tapped the boy's shoulder for approval.
-I think a small group will have a better chance of success, Mostaggeda knows the region.
- I would also like to participate; I don't have anything to do in the Great River- Mumny intervene.
It was decided, most of the group would return to the Great River, transporting the wounded.
The four warriors were preparing to follow in Agga's footsteps.

THE VICTORY OF THE MOON'S CLAN

The wooden Goddess seemed indifferent to that group of brutal-looking warriors gathered around the stone altar.
Certain stones found in the desert were crushed into a powder that, mixed with water, was used to bleach surfaces. With them they had painted the altar with an intense white, the symbol of lunar light. The light of two torches, installed in the base of the Altar, highlighted the color, giving an unreal aspect to the whole.
Agga uttered a guttural battle cry by lifting the ivory spear in the direction of the altar.
-Victory, Clan of the Moon!
He was standing on a small platform of logs and skins, haranguing his men. In spite of the defeat, he felt powerful again; he had a force of little more than forty warriors.
The cacique's face was painted ochre and several eagle feathers stood out over his head, Agga's figure, under the undulating light of the bonfires, looked frightening, imposing, making a strong impression on his men.
With his herring, the chieftain managed to spread his wild determination to the group of warriors.

The slaves should prepare the fermented drink for the next full moon; everything was ready for the celebration that would celebrate the arrival of the Goddess, after the supposed victory.

Agga, Susuda and the rest of the surviving group had taken the utmost care not to reveal the serious defeat. Nevertheless, the slaves, their children, and the group that did not participate in the expedition wondered why so many men had disappeared in a single raid. What really happened?

Despite the doubts, the unpredictable brutality of Susuda and his henchmen had avoided inconvenient questions.

Fifteen days after the river defeat, five days had passed since the warriors had returned to the village... the enemy had not yet appeared.

The cacique's initial fear was turning into a sense of victory.

-They will not come. After the combat they have returned to the Great River.

Overflowing with pride, Agga regained her optimism.

- They barely intended to rescue their women - he declared, euphoric.

However, Susuda was still worried, he often wondered:

-Why didn't they attack us? What are they planning?

The four warriors arrived that afternoon at the oasis that marked the beginning of the territory of the Red-Haired Men. Two days ago they were separated from the rest of the group, which undertook the return to the Great River.

Hor knew that place in detail, there he defeated an enemy sentry some time ago, the remains of the skeleton were still visible, torn apart by jackals or hyenas.

Ashes and some charred logs revealed the funeral pyres of the Red-haired Man.

Hor quenched thirst in the small lake.

- Nungal also drank, filling a bladder with the precious liquid.

- We won't catch up with them before they reach their destination, eh?

Hor watched the vast plain; on the horizon one could guess the surface of the lake with its bluish tones in contrast to the aridity of the territory.

-We haven't found any remains of bonfires that indicate that they feed during the march, and sleep for short periods, that way they managed to extend the advantage.

-Then we won't be able to reach them.

Mostaggeda agreed.

-Agga will remain alert for the first few days after the return. Possibly he has placed sentries along the way; it seemed strange to me that I had not found one in this oasis.

-Refugees in their village, after six or seven days they will feel safe again.

-Then he will withdraw his sentries, at least most of them.

Mostaggeda stretched out on the grass, his hands under his head.

-No doubt he will celebrate it in the same way as he celebrated previous victories.
-Victory? -Nungal smiled sarcastically - How do they celebrate their victories?
-Drinking a potion that plunges them into a kind of madness, they lose their senses, some sleep for a whole day, they stagger, and they can't get up.
Everyone was extremely interested in the young man's story.
-It was during such a feast that, together with Menuttaui, I took the opportunity to escape.
-When do you suppose they should celebrate the victory?
- Are you sure they will celebrate? - It seemed to be something absurd - because in reality they received a tremendous beating.
-I know him well, he will transform the defeat into a supposed victory, and he will justify the casualties with some lie, I think he will use the statue of the goddess to support his story.
Nungal insisted on his question:
-When do you think he will celebrate?
-Oh, ten or twenty days after his return, during the next Full Moon. Agga's main ambition is to consolidate his authority over all the clans of the great lake region, for that he needs victories.
- We have enough time, which would be the perfect time to attack them.
- There is one detail that I have not yet mentioned - added Mostaggeda - during the banquet they feed on human flesh.
They all turned to the young redheaded warrior.
-Are they cannibals? They devour their slaves?
-They usually consume the bodies of people they capture in their raids; I never saw them do it with their slaves.
There was a silence; suddenly everyone calculated the chances of being captured alive by Red-Haired Men. Guessing his thoughts, the young man smiled.
-You mustn't worry, my friends. Under the effects of the drink they will be vulnerable.

At dawn the group descended from the hills to the great lake.
Hor knew the territory, guiding his companions along the same path he had traveled some time before. Three days later they reached the margin. They had found no sign of the enemy, apparently feeling confident, as Mostaggeda supposed.
The village of the Red-haired Men was a few hours to the south, when they were preparing to camp on the shore of the lake, a lonely light in the distance denounced the human presence.
-It must be a sentry, possibly two warriors.
- Sentinels who light bonfires, revealing their position?

-Perhaps it's as Mostaggeda calculated, they feel safe.
- We must dominate them tonight, it will be impossible to do it by day.
They walked cautiously for a little more than half an hour, as they approached they noticed that the fire was on the edge of the lake, on flat ground with little vegetation.
Lying on the ground, the four warriors examined the place. At a distance of one kilometer, they could see the solitary silhouette of an individual sitting in front of the fire.
-I think one of us could crawl there unnoticed.
Nungal was upset, something wasn't right.
-He doesn't look like a sentry, is he a fisherman?
Mostaggeda also hesitated - They never place sentries in the open, they usually hide in woods or hills.
-Can't we just ignore it and leave it behind?
-It wouldn't be smart to leave a free enemy in our rear.
Hor and Nungal decided to approach; their companions remained watching the rear.
The young men separated, crawling carefully to cover the individual from both sides. The Moon had not yet appeared on the horizon, an intense darkness was hiding them, and they managed to reach a distance of less than two hundred meters. The night breeze might denounce their presence, but at that height the sentry would no longer escape.
They stood to converge directly to the bonfire. The sentry was a young man of Red Hair, who rose quickly to see two warriors walking in his direction. Hor noted that the man had no spear, barely wielding a dagger. Reaching less than ten meters, he commanded in a firm voice
 -Drop that dagger! - The guy didn't move - you didn't understand me? - With a gesture he pointed towards the hand of the individual, who seemed to guess the order, because he lowered his arm, without letting go of the knife. Five meters behind the enemy, with his bow ready, Nungal was undecided.
 -What do we do now, should I shoot him?
At that moment they heard screams from the darkness, they recognized the voices of Mumny and Mostaggeda, along with others in the language of the enemy.
Hor and Nungal kept the sentry under the threat of their bows, though their attention was directed to their friends who were running towards them.
-It's an ambush! - Mostaggeda shouted. As he stopped by the campfire he immediately recognized the sentry. The giant Mumny stood beside his friends, panting from the swift race.
-Hemman, what are you doing here?
He was one of his best friends, whom he used to meet at night to divide stolen goods and tell stories.

- Mostaggeda, forgive me, those bastards forced me. I didn't know you would come with the enemy.

The four young men concentrated all their attention on the darkness of the plain, where the diffuse shadows of several men walked in their direction. It would be impossible to try to shoot their arrows, dazzled by the light of the bonfire.

-We must get out of the clarity, it's impossible to try to fight here!

At that moment the ambush was completed, behind their backs six Red-Haired Men, who had remained hidden in the lake, hurriedly hurled themselves at the four young men. Hor turned quickly with an arrow, but the short distance hurt his aim. The arrow was lost in the darkness and fell into the lake. Mumny wielded his short spear ready to resist to the end, Mostaggeda turned the sling by his side. Hor, who was closer to the lake, was immediately knocked down by two heavy warriors who held his arms. They had not used their spears, the young man understood; they were trying to capture them alive!

The warriors coming from the darkness surrounded the group pointing their long spears at a short distance from the young men, Mostaggeda stopped, it would be useless to try to resist.

Mumny and Nungal felt the heavy tips of the enemy spears leaning on their bodies. The black archer had not fired his deadly arrows as he was overtaken by the swift enemy action. He felt a strong hand seize his bow.

Hor summed up the feeling of all - We have allowed ourselves to be captured as a gang of children.

In the darkness of the night the group set out. Twelve Red-Haired warriors escorted their four captives who walked with their arms tied behind their backs. A long rod was attached with thick leather straps to each prisoner's neck, keeping the captives in line. Mumny's tall stature hampered the movements of Nungal, which preceded him.

The victorious warriors walked proudly commenting on the action, examining the famous arrows of the black warriors, trying to understand the mystery of their power. The young Hemman managed to walk close to Mostaggeda without attracting the attention of the warriors.

- A sentry warned you two days ago, knowing that you were a small group, they prepared the ambush.

- We let ourselves be surprised as children - Mostaggeda lamented again.

 -They said you had been the leader of a rebellion, murdering old Turahena and his friends.

-That's not true; I just wanted to avenge my mother's death!

-They said you died trying to escape.

A warrior struck a blow with the end of his spear on Mostaggeda's head.

-Silence, bastard! - The young man looked at him angrily, the warrior replied with an ironic giggle.

- Susuda reserves a special punishment for you, mongrel - A second warrior, walking with the spear on his shoulder, intervened - You can say goodbye to your friends, soon we will have a full moon - Mostaggeda assumed that his friends had not understood the words of his captors, because they were marching in silence. Hemman stepped forward; he would avoid talking to his friend for the rest of the journey.
Two hours later they arrived at the village of the Moon Clan.

The captives were tied to solid wooden posts inside the caves on the rocky wall. They were within a short distance of each other; they could see each other and talk discreetly. Outside, protected by the shadow of the wall, a boring sentry watched over the prisoners. Each captive, despite being tied up, could make limited movements that allowed him to feed and drink using only one arm. From day one, with the exception of Mostaggeda, the prisoners destined for the cannibalistic banquet received food and water in abundance.
Noticing that the young redhead was not fed in the same way, the boys managed to give him part of their food.
 Mostaggeda knew that he would be the only captive not destined to be devoured. That meant no privilege, his fate would likely be terrifying, as Susuda would insinuate shortly thereafter.
From where he stood, Hor examined the village. To his left were many circular huts, interspersed with palm trees and some trees. A little further on, toward the center of the village, a small circular stone wall surrounded a water fountain, located where the open esplanade, the villagers' meeting place began.
The wide square extended to the right, up to a large bonfire that burned permanently. Beside the fire had raised a mound of rocks, logs and skins. Above was a statue depicting a female figure with a beetle in hands. On both sides of the statue he could see two torches, usually lit at night. The young man understood that she was the goddess of the Nungal clan. He glanced at the black warrior, who seemed to sleep, sitting with his back resting on the post.
A little further on, Mostaggeda was also observing the village. He had been struck by the presence of small groups of young people who circulated at all times near the caves. They seemed to be doing normal work, sometimes carrying firewood or going to the well to fetch water. Mostaggeda sensed that they were looking furtively in his direction. He knew some of them; they were young men whom the Red-Haired Men regarded as bastards. With those boys he shared many moments of suffering in the past. They did not address him with gestures or words, it was not necessary. Like their parents, they could understand each other at a glance.
The sound of footsteps interrupted their thoughts. A group of warriors, led by Agga, approached the grotto. The chieftain walked with both hands behind his

back. Beside him, Susuda directed a hate-filled gaze at Mostaggeda. The group stopped in front of Nungal, which seemed to awaken.
Susuda kicked Mostaggeda's leg.
-Can you communicate with them?
-Yes, I can translate your words using my mother's dialect. Is that what you want, you fucking coward?
Agga held back the warrior who was already lifting his spear. Going to Nungal, he began to speak, calmly.
-All of you will be sacrificed to our gods on the Full Moon, it's a great honor for you, swamp worms - he pointed his finger directly at Nungal - however there is a way to save your miserable life - He paused so that Mostaggeda could translate his words. Nungal listened without showing emotion, his eyes fixed on the cacique. Agga withdrew his hands from his back, lifting a small arrow adorned by a red feather.
-What is the secret of these arrows?
A sarcastic smile illuminated for an instant the face of the black warrior - It's magical - Upon hearing the translation, Agga replied - I offer you life in exchange for that magic. Nungal tried to gain time - it's a ritual that must be executed after the Full Moon - Susuda moved impatiently - He's mocking you, Agga, let me torture him, I will tear the truth out of him!
Agga did not answer, he had seen many tortured people die without revealing their secrets, and he did not trust Susuda's ability in that sense.
-You have until the eve of the Full Moon to save your life.
The other captives were of no importance to Agga, who only glanced indifferently briefly at Hor before turning around to leave. Susuda pointed a threatening finger at Mostaggeda.
-For you I have reserved a special destiny, damned bastard.
When the group left, Hor went to Nungal.
-What are you trying to do with this magic story?
-I don't know, maybe buy time.
-If those monsters had poisoned arrows, it would be a disaster for all the inhabitants of the Great River - Nungal smiled again.
- Do you think I'll reveal the secret?
Mumny shook the post to which he was tied.
-We must escape!
-It won't be so easy; they're watching us day and night.
-The Full Moon is five days away!
From his position, Mostaggeda exchanged an enigmatic glance with two Red-Haired young men who at that moment were walking in front of the huts, carrying a long road from which some fish hung.

Silence reigned in the village, most of its inhabitants slept. The Moon had hidden a few minutes ago and the shadows took over the night.
Without understanding the cause, Hor suddenly awoke, all his senses were attentive to what was happening in the vicinity. The sentry slept soundly, sitting on the ground with his back resting on the rock, a short distance from the entrance to the grotto. The gentle rubbing caused by the stealthy steps of a shadow sliding in the darkness caught his attention. He lifted his head trying to delve into the darkness.
A silhouette stood out as he walked toward the grotto. Without a doubt, someone approached the post where Mostaggeda was.
For a moment Hor thought of shouting denouncing the intruder, because he thought it was an attempt to assassinate his friend, but he discarded the thought when he saw that Mostaggeda was awake and straightened his body to speak in whispers with the shadow leaning beside him. Apparently no one was sleeping, because the young redhead gestured to Mumny to remain silent. The silhouette seemed to argue with Mostaggeda using the language of the Red-Haired Men, they whispered for a few minutes. Finally, he slipped into the shadows, disappearing into the night.
Guessing the eager curiosity of his companions, Mostaggeda turned to whoever was closest, Mumny listened attentively.
-Tomorrow they will try to free us all, we must be prepared.
-Who is this mysterious ally?
-They are my old friends, the sons of the slaves, rejected by the clan. When the Moon hides, they will try to cut our moorings and guide us out of the village, avoiding the northern sentry.
-Why hasn't he done it now, when he had the chance? - Mumny was exalted.
-There is a condition; they want to know if we accept them in our village on the Great River, after helping us they will suffer serious reprisals if they stay here.
From its pole, the voice of Nungal was heard, accompanying the dialogue.
- We accept them, of course, they will be welcome to the clan - Mostaggeda raised his free arm.
-In that case... tomorrow we'll get out of here!

Agga listened in silence to an angry Susuda who moved describing circles in front of the stone where the chieftain was sitting.
As usual, they had moved away from the village that morning to discuss in particular, away from indiscreet listeners. Under the shade of a palm tree, Susuda explained the reasons for his anger.
-I ask only for one life, it's little in exchange for all the support I have always given you.
-Can't you wait until the night of the banquet?

-That nigger will never reveal his secret if you don't really threaten him!
-He knows that he will be sacrificed on the night of the Full Moon.
Susuda raised his voice impatiently - He's a warrior, he does not fear death!
Agga reflected, he needed to know the secret of those deadly arrows.
-Why do you think that by executing her friend in advance we will succeed?
-We won't execute him immediately; I intend to tear him apart little by little in front of the group.
Agga calculated the effect that it might have on the slaves, their children, and all those who were not directly part of his group. Many did not approve of the death of old Turahena, and he did not wish to increase the tension in the clan... at least until he knew the power of those deadly arrows.
-Two days to the Full Moon - Agga reflected for a moment - you can do it, you have my consent!
Susuda drew a satisfied smile, but the chief warned, whispering - But you must solve everything discreetly and quickly, you will interrogate the captive outside the village.
-I am free to proceed in my own way?
Agga gave in -Torture and execute the half-breed as you see fit, if you think that will loosen the tongue of that black man.
Susuda shook his head satisfied; finally he would give his due to that bastard who had the audacity to assassinate a member of the group during the previous banquet.
Agga murmured, apparently thinking aloud -It would have a great effect on our people if I revealed my new weapons that night, while I proclaim the Goddess of the Beetle, who left the Great River to protect us.

In the grotto, the captives waited anxiously for the arrival of night. Mostaggeda had communicated that morning to the young allies Nungal's answer, accepting to receive them in the clan. The boy did not need to say a word, a simple nod had sufficed. The young conspirator, who was supplying water at the fountain, responded to the prisoner's gesture with a poorly concealed smile, before withdrawing with a quick step.
If he had taken a few minutes to leave, he would have seen the group of three warriors walking slowly to the grotto. Susuda gestured toward Mostaggeda. The young man imagined it was another interrogation trying to uncover the secret of the arrows, but when he saw that they were releasing him from the post, forcing him to stand, he understood the gravity of his situation.
When he was led to Susuda, who was waiting outside, he assumed that he would be executed. Without saying a word, the warrior dropped a heavy blow on the young man's face, which did not collapse because his captors held him by the arms.

The punishment was repeated in silence for a few minutes. Seeing that Susuda would not stop, the captives began to scream, demanding an end to the torture. They insulted the fearless warrior who now struck with a flexible stick, marking the torso of the young unconscious. The sudden turmoil caught the attention of the village and many heads peeked into each hut. A young redhead dropped the wood he was carrying to run to the meadow where a group of boys worked. Some people approached Susuda, demonstrating their indignation with shouts and gestures. Agga watched in silence from inside her hut, Susuda did not obey her demand to act discreetly. It was a serious mistake, the situation could become complicated because people did not see Mostaggeda as an enemy, and they considered him as a member of the clan, so he should not be tortured.
-If he's guilty he must be executed, you cannot torture him!
-Why don't you torture the other prisoners? They are our real enemies!
-Release Mostaggeda! He has done no harm to anyone; he barely defended himself from a murderer!
Susuda stopped, sweating profusely.
Unlike Agga, he was not impressed by the screams; he knew that his men would be by his side, ready to defend him.
A warrior approached to speak quietly.
- You better take him away from the village to execute him; it's an order from Agga!
Susuda glanced at the cacique's hut; a simple exchange of glances was enough.
-Move the prisoner to the reed, to the edge of the lake, and wait for me.
With a fast pace Susuda went to his hut, followed by the hostile gaze of some people.

After the cool waters of the lake returned his consciousness, Mostaggeda shook his confused head, slowly remembering what had happened.
He felt strong pains all over his body, his face had swollen, he bled from several cuts. When he looked up, he saw two warriors standing by his side, they seemed to be waiting impatiently, watching at all times towards the village, about four hundred meters away. He understood that he had been dragged there to be executed. Near his hand, at the edge of the water, there was a good-sized stone, which he could use as a weapon. Observing the robust bearing of his guardians, he calculated that he would accomplish nothing with a simple stone.
At that moment he heard one of the warriors exclaim in an authoritative voice.
-You have nothing to do here, leave or you will regret it!
As he turned he saw six young men approaching, the warriors stepped forward to keep Mostaggeda out of reach of the intruders and lifted their spears.

Mostaggeda was apparently without the strength to rise, yet he clutched the stone firmly when he heard someone approaching from the other flank, running towards the warriors to attack them from behind.

The guards also listened and tried to turn around, but it was too late, a spear stuck in the belly of one of them.

At the same time, the group began to throw stones and some clubs on the surviving warrior, who, cornered, was blindly stabbing his spear trying to stop his aggressors.

Mostaggeda took advantage of the confusion by jumping to his feet and crashing the stone into the warrior's skull, which shrank and immediately received numerous blows. It was all over when a spear was buried in his chest.

As he watched the spearman, Mostaggeda was surprised.

-Hemman!

-Come on, there's no time to lose!

The boy was struggling to remove the spear from the body of the defeated warrior.

Mostaggeda picked up a spear from the fallen, before running after his rescuers.

-What will happen to my fellow captives?

-We'll see later. First we must get you to safety.

Hiding in the unevenness of the terrain, they headed south, outlining the lake.

Shortly afterwards Susuda discovered the bloody bodies of his men.

With a quick glance he interpreted the footprints in the sand.

He ran back to the village, Agga went to meet him.

-Has he been executed?

No! - Exclaimed the warrior - He has fled, he received help from some people, my men are dead!

Agga was perplexed; exactly what he feared was happening.

-They have been his bastard friends.

- Give me five men and in one day I'll bring their heads.

-It's what I feared; the clan threatens to rise up.

-Agga, you're the chief, you must order the capture of these bastards!

-No, we can't chase them now, I need everyone here tomorrow. We must show unity during the feast of the Full Moon. You can't be absent.

-We have not yet discovered the secret of the arrows. I'm just asking you for a morning alone with that nigger and I'll make him talk!

-No, I had an idea. We must change the ceremony to gain time.

Susuda stopped, with the spear in her hand.

-What are you talking about?

-We won't execute them in advance, as usual. We'll do it during the ceremony, we must skin them right there, one by one, before placing them for roasting.

Susuda shook his head; he had understood the macabre plan of his chief.
-You intend to leave the black man in last place, forcing him to witness the death of his friends.
-If he decides to speak, he will find salvation, otherwise he will be devoured.
-He will speak; he will loosen his tongue to save himself!
- And he will really be saved... at least for that night.
-We will discreetly eliminate him later.
Both agreed; they could still discover the secret that would give them the coveted power.

Pessimism took hold of the captives. They assumed that Mostaggeda had been executed that afternoon. After dark, they waited anxiously all night, but no one appeared. The captives imagined that, with Mostaggeda's death, the group intended to help them had given up their plans.

Mumny stopped, his arms bled from the tremendous effort made, for hours he had tried to tear off the post to which he was tied, but all had been in vain, the high column stood firm. Exhausted, sweating profusely, he let himself fall to the ground.

That night, the last of their lives, no one slept.

The three prisoners were awake when the faint clarity on the horizon announced a new day.

A small crowd gathered in the village of the Red-Haired Men, they had lit several bonfires around the central esplanade, where most of those warriors converged. During the day some groups had arrived from the northern territories of the lake. The main bonfire was already raising its flames, which illuminated the statue of the Goddess, towards which the curious glances of the visitors were directed. They had decorated it with wreaths of flowers, feathers, colorful pebbles, shells and snails, two slaves proceeded to light the torches of the altar.
The Goddess seemed to raise the sacred beetle with a threatening gesture toward those men who dared to remove her from their home, her disturbing gaze shone in the dancing light of the torches. A row of small logs, intended to be used as seats, had been arranged describing a wide circle around the bonfire. Huge turtle shells containing fermented beverage, which had been distributed among the seats, completed the stage of the banquet.
Everything was arranged.
It was dusk. In a cloudless sky the Full Moon loomed over the horizon. In his hut Agga felt euphoric. A leopard skin covered his shoulders, falling down his back

like a cape. A strip of leather, adorned with fangs of the same feline, held the skin in place. Vulture feathers adorned the cacique's head.
Susuda and a couple of very young warriors waited for him at the entrance to the hut. Proudly grasping the ivory spear, Agga appeared at the door, smiling at his companions. Susuda gestured broadly at the teenagers.
-They are the best specimens of our race, selected to guard you up to the altar.
The presence of the young people at the ceremony was important, exhibiting the physical characteristics of their people. Susuda wanted to emphasize the bastard character of the group of rebellious youth; he knew that what happened the day before would be commented by his visitors.
The problems with the rejected children were not exclusive to the clan of Agga, they affected the whole race, for that reason the cacique tried to exhibit those privileged young people, worthy representatives of the future of the clan.
At that time, some warriors led the three captives to the center of the village. They walked through the crowd, stopping in front of three stakes, where they were tied up.
The captives remained silent, because a guard, a short distance away, struck them with a long stick when they tried to talk to each other. Nungal and Mumny looked insistently at the statue of their Goddess, possibly implored for help.
Agga and his small retinue emerged on the esplanade, as they passed the crowd of warriors cheering for the "victorious" chieftain, who walked slowly in the direction of the small platform he used to harangue his people.
As he climbed up he lifted the spear with a triumphant gesture, the warriors responded with a hoarse war cry, waving their fists. As usual, no one carried spears or clubs during the ceremony, they could barely carry their daggers, which they would use to cut meat. All weapons would be kept in a hut.
- My warriors!
A loud acclamation answered.
- O invincible warriors! Conquerors! Look - he pointed the spear at the statue - The gods of the enemy have submitted to our power!
The chieftain clenched the fist of his left hand, threatening.
-Even the most distant people fear us; the villages of the Great River have been consumed under the flames of our wrath!
The crowd seemed to go mad, shouting the name of the chief - Agga! Agga! Agga!
- He waited for a few minutes satisfied, until there was silence.
-Do you know why we triumphed? Because we are united! United we are powerful!
He glanced quickly at Susuda, who offered him a great snail.
-Brothers, drink with me. Drink to celebrate victory.
The banquet was beginning; the prisoners understood that the time had come. Susuda approached Nungal with a small arrow in her hand.

105

-It's your last chance to save your life.
 The young man did not understand the words, but he clearly understood their meaning.
 -Do you know what you can do with that arrow? Susuda did not understand either, assumed that Nungal was revealing the secret to him, and approached the prisoner, demonstrating his anxiety.
-What did you say?
 He hadn't foreseen that, he needed a translator!
Hor understood the situation.
 -Damn monster, go to hell - the smile and the kind expression of his face did not reveal the meaning of his words, Nungal dispelled the last doubts of the warrior by making an affirmative gesture with his head.
-They want to talk, we've done it!
Susuda mumbled a dry order to the guardian, who immediately left.
The captives had gained time.
All over the esplanade, people drank among great laughter; some already exhibited the first effects of drunkenness, looking impatiently at the bonfire.
-Where is the meat?
 Susuda went sarcastically to Hor.
 - You will be the first, I don't need you.
 Agga had descended from the platform, with a huge snail in his hand, he approached.
-They are impatient; we must sacrifice the first victim.
 The guardian returned at that moment, accompanied by two slaves with long black hair, Susuda pointed to the captives.
-The woman looked at Nungal.
-Do you understand me, warrior?
Nungal understood perfectly, it was the same dialect with which Hor expressed himself, at the same time he noticed something strange, the slave seemed to be extremely nervous, she avoided looking directly at the young son of the chief Arnut.
The second slave addressed Nungal with an indifferent tone.
-When it all begins, we will try to cut your ties.
That was a real surprise, Nungal made an effort not to reveal any emotion.
-What did you say?
The first slave winked at Mumny, muttering in a calm voice.
-I hope you are not only enormous, but also fast, warrior.
A short distance away, behind the women's backs, Susuda and Agga had not understood those words, the second slave shrugged in discouragement. She turned to Susuda.
-He hasn't answered me, I'm sorry.

Agga was impatient - We are wasting time! - Among the crowd someone exclaimed, visibly intoxicated:
-Shall we eat them or chat with them?
Susuda decided to increase the pressure on the prisoners.
-We must sacrifice the first.
Susuda looked at the guardian, nodding, and the man cut Hor's ropes.
The boy looked at his companions in silence.
They led him behind the altar; two men waited wielding long flint knives.
Hor could see a T-shaped pole, where his body would be hung shortly after to be flayed. That thought made him react, he tried to surprise the guardian, pushing him with his shoulder. It was useless; it was a veteran warrior who seemed to know many tricks, with an ironic chuckle the man held the young man by one arm, dragging him to the place of sacrifice.
It was the end.
Hor let himself be led; his arms were tied over his head.
He watched the man approach with a dagger.
He closed his eyes in anticipation of the deadly blow.

Hor could not tell how long he remained closed-eyed, probably only a few seconds, though it seemed like an eternity to him.
Then he heard a strange guttural sound.
As he looked up, he saw that the man had released the dagger and looked at him with his exorbitant eyes, his body shuddering.
A long arrow pierced his throat.
Without giving them time to react, several arrows hit the executioners.
Curiously, they seemed to suffer the effects of some kind of poison that the young man was unaware of, they vomited before falling, shaken by frightening riles.
Suddenly, Hor found himself in the middle of a real battle; warriors emerged from all sides attacking the crowd on the esplanade.
The shouting was infernal, the young man shook himself trying to get rid of the moorings, when a silhouette slid beside him, she was the slave who spoke to him shortly before.
The woman bent down to take the executioner's knife, cutting the leather straps that bound Hor's arms.
Feeling free, the boy held the woman by her shoulders.
-Thank you, don't leave here, I'll try to release my friends.
Armed with the dagger he ran towards the fire, as he approached he could see that his friends were already liberated by warriors of familiar appearance, carrying triangular shields.
Nungal already wielded a short spear, Mumny smiled sarcastically at his side as he saw him.

- Well, for the one who has just been sacrificed, you look good!
Someone held him a spear, while holding it, Hor discovered that it was Taklamakan.
-What hole did you come from, man?
Taklamakan didn't have time to answer; he had thrown an arrow at a robust redheaded warrior who suddenly stopped, vomiting before collapsing.
The crowd gathered in that confined space was a temptation to the archers, a rain of arrows falling on them. Whoever tried to escape was stopped by a wall of lancers that ruthlessly eliminated him.
On the esplanade, drunken men lay unconscious among the corpses. It had been a fulminant attack.
Among the attackers, Nungal discovered some young redheads participating in the fight, when a figure approached; he lifted the spear but interrupted the movement when he identified it.
- Mostaggeda!
The young man smiled with difficulty, because of the face deformed by the blows received.
- Hello Nungal, we were afraid we'd be too late.
The Red-Haired Men were practically unarmed, barely disposing of their knives, so the resistance quickly ceased.
Nungal went with a group towards the hut of Agga, trying to find the cacique. Inside there was no one, but the young man recovered his small bow and the dreaded arrows.
On his way out, he gave Mumny his guns. Smiling, the giant warrior kissed his bow.
-You can't imagine how much I've missed you, my dear.

When the first cries of alarm were heard, Agga and Susuda were near the captives and their reaction had been swift.
Veterans of numerous battles, they quickly headed for Susuda's hut. The arrows fell on the esplanade; Agga rejected two warriors who tried to get in his way, using his ivory spear. Susuda entered the hut to leave immediately, carrying his heavy spear. Some warriors joined their chiefs, it was necessary to organize the defense.
Witnessing the effects of those arrows, Agga knew that all was lost, without saying a word, he disappeared behind the hut.
Susuda concentrated all his attention on the defense, so he did not perceive the escape of the cacique.
On the esplanade, the fight came to an end.

Nungal, Mostaggeda and Mumny, with a group of archers, emerged in front of Susuda and his men. There was no combat; the arrows quickly eliminated the warriors. Susuda stood between the dying bodies of her group.
He showed no fear, his gaze was defiant, as he examined the enemy group facing him he discovered Mostaggeda.
-You! Damn you!
He shouted a hateful cry, lifting the spear to run towards the young man.
Nungal had his small bow ready.
-Did you want my arrows? Here's one.
The little arrow sank into Susuda's belly, which stopped the race, and he startled at the red feathers, staggering. White foam erupted from his mouth, he fell to his knees and his head hung over his chest.
The mighty Susuda was dead.
 Mostaggeda gazed at the corpse for a moment, and then walked toward the esplanade.

Agga slipped behind the huts, hiding in the shadows. The lake could offer him shelter, walking into the water he would move away from the village.
But for that, he had to cross a hundred meters of open terrain.
He had taken his first steps when a voice from the shadows stopped him.
-Agga!
As he turned he discovered the young white-skinned prisoner, wielding a short spear. That young man did not represent a threat to a strong warrior, veteran of so many combats. The chieftain attacked in silence, firmly wielding his ivory spear.
Hor had enough time during his captivity to get to know the small village in detail. From the grotto he could examine the entire place, so it was not difficult for him to guess the cacique's escape route. The young man recognized his father's spear in Agga's hands, when he dodged the first thrust by turning the body.
Despite his robust and heavy body, the chieftain was agile, moving skillfully, launching a series of stabs that did not allow his opponent to counterattack. Hor defended himself from the blows, understood that he was fighting the way his opponent preferred, body to body, so he could not prevent a blow from opening a long wound in his left arm. Agga was in a hurry, he needed to finish that boy, before other enemies arose. Hor began to feel the effects of that rain of blows, his breath became agitated, and the sweat covered his face.
With a quick movement Agga opened a second wound on Hor's left leg.
Seeing Hor begin to retreat with a frightened expression, Agga set out to deliver the final blow. At that moment the young man ran with difficulty toward the village. Apparently he was on the run.

-Fucking coward, come back here!
Agga hesitated for a moment; he should follow the enemy to liquidate him, risking to be discovered by other warriors, or took advantage to escape?
A distance of three meters separated the contenders when Hor suddenly stopped and turned around lifting his spear.
 Agga understood that the young man did not flee, he barely needed space to counterattack, and he remained indecisive for a brief moment that was fatal to the chieftain.
The spear flew in his direction. With a dry sound, it reached the cacique's chest; Agga uttered a loud cry of pain and collapsed from behind.
After a brief agony, her body stopped shaking.
Agga was dead.
Hor must have struggled to remove the spear from the cacique's hand, tightly closed.
Bleeding from his wounds, he walked back to the village with difficulty.
He sat down on a log to drink directly from a turtle shell; the fermented drink seemed to alleviate the pain. A slave came quietly to take care of her wounds. In a few minutes the woman stagnated the blood on her leg, and examined her arm, when the boy received a pleasant surprise.
-Hello, hunter - At the familiar female voice, Hor turned quickly, standing indifferent to the pain.
-Menuttaui!
The girl hugged him; they remained in that position for several minutes.
 - How is that possible?
On his back the woman pushed him by the arm, forcing him to sit down, to continue treating his wounds. Menuttaui helped her.
 Nungal and Mostaggeda sat down a short distance away, looking extremely tired. A little further back, near the altar, Mumny had improvised a mattress with some skins and was already sleeping soundly. Taklamakan smiled incredulously.
-How can he sleep in the midst of all this madness?
Some slaves with white skin and long black hair approached Hor and Menuttaui, offering them food and water. One of them asked with a smile:
-How are you, young chief?
-Chief? - Nungal was surprised - Are you the leader of your clan?
- Leader of a disjointed clan - he smiled bitterly - with half of my people enslaved.
-And you agreed to settle with yours in my village- sighed Nungal- That will be a dilemma, how can I be the chieftain of a chieftain?
-I confess that at first I thought the same thing - he embraced Menuttaui - now it doesn't seem important to me, I just want to form a family in peace.
The freed slaves surrounded the couple.
- Akrabuamelu Arnut's son cannot be anyone's vassal.
-Akrabuamelu Hor is our chief- exclaimed another young woman.

Nungal smiled openly, liked to feel the intensity of the ties that united that group, did not want to lose the friendship of this brave young man.

-We'll solve everything in due time, don't worry.

In the esplanade the victors organized the village, helped by many young people of Red Hair. There was no fire or looting, that was not an expedition of thieves, and they had barely extirpated the Evil that plagued the region.

Seeing the approach of a group, Taklamakan muttered, smiling.

-Here comes our mighty commander.

-Kutum?

The old man approached with a broad smile, partially hidden by his long white beard.

- Hello Chief, how are you? - Pointing to Mumny- Is he hurt?

-No, just tired, he hasn't slept for a few days.

Hor gently pushed Menuttaui aside, allowing the slave to take care of his arm wound.

-Once and for all, could someone explain to me how you came?

The young woman smiled - It's simple, when the warriors returned to the delta, they informed us that you would attack the enemy village, Ziuzu decided to imitate the daring of the enemy.

Taklamakan continued the young woman's account.

-The chieftain organized a fleet of canoes. We sailed the sea for two days. Interrogating the fishermen of the coast, we discovered where to disembark and the way to the village.

-By a stroke of luck, we found Mostaggeda's group, who informed us about the fate these monsters reserved for you.

Nungal examined a completely different arrow.

-I have seen the enemies die after vomiting, what is that?

Kutum placed his hands on his waist, with a proud gesture.

-From the first day I witnessed the effect of your arrows, I dedicated myself to creating a different poison.

-I imagined that everything must be your work.

-After several failures, based on the ointment I applied to Ziuzu's head, I managed to develop a potion that mixes snake venom with... well, with other little things.

-They die vomiting, it's disgusting - Exclaimed Taklamakan.

Two days later, the group returned, walking towards the sea. Mostaggeda said goodbye to his friends, he had decided to stay with his people in the village. Free from their oppressors, the new clan would open up to the neighboring villages, without slaves, they wanted to live in peace.

They intended to maintain strong trade ties with the inhabitants of the Great River.

Over time, perhaps their race would evolve into completely different peoples, the basis of future civilizations.

EPILOGUE

The Great River ran slowly, measuring time by eras, indifferent to the human drama on its banks. The village had been rebuilt on the hill next to the river, surrounded by a strong palisade of logs. More than forty circular huts revealed its prosperity.

In the center of the village rose a high promontory of stones, visible from the river. The small pier had been enlarged, and crocodiles could no longer be seen in the vicinity. Many canoes remained moored between the papyruses.

In the space separating the village from the river, bonfires slowly roasted the meat of some animals, carefully cared for by the elderly, surrounded by children and dogs. Little Gen seemed to have adapted perfectly to the new home, running through the trees, noisily accompanied by his friends and pets. A small crowd filled the space between the huts.

The great Ziuzu seemed happy among the group of fishermen and warriors, smiling as he stroked his huge belly with his hands. At his side the old man Kutum spoke about potions, diets and fermented drinks.

A group of warriors, some with black skin, others wearing long black hair on very light skin, carefully transported the statue of the Goddess, under the attentive gaze of the clan. After making sure that the figure remained in a firm position, they descended from the altar to join the villagers.

Arising on one side of the altar, Hor and Nungal solemnly walked a few steps to stop, side by side. Both wore leopard skins, carrying the ceremonial spears with their characteristic ivory tips in their hands. Nungal's spear bore the figure of a beetle, in contrast to Hor's scorpion. There were no warrior harangues, both young men contemplating their people smiling in silence. That would be the first village ruled by two chiefs in perfect harmony, trading in peace with their neighbors, open to receive the nomads who left the arid lands of the west.

Ziuzu raised an open hand in the direction of the new chiefs.

-Hail, my friends. Akrabuamelu Hor and Akrabuamelu Nungal, sons of the Scorpion and the Beetle! Hail! Hail! Hail!

A legend was being born. Fat Ziuzu tapped his elbow slightly at the old Kutum, who stood beside him.

-You must get an insect to be my protector, I find it very pretty.

-In your case, don't you think a hippopotamus would be more appropriate?

THE END

TRILOGY ADVENTURES IN THE PALEOLITHIC

-CLANS AT WAR
-THE QUEEN OF THE NEANDERTHALS
-SANCTUARY

AND BY THE SAME AUTHOR

-LOST IN THE AMERICAS
-THE ORIGIN OF LIFE
-FROM DINOSAURS TO MAMMALS
-FROM PRIMATES TO HUMANS
-PREHISTORIC AMERICAS
-THE WORLD IN 2500-2000 BC
-THE TIMES ATLAS OF THE ANCIENT HISTORY

Milton Keynes UK
Ingram Content Group UK Ltd.
UKHW012305141124
451150UK00011B/183